THE CHINESE ZODIAC MYSTERY

By

J.D. MALLINSON

Waxwing Books, New Hampshire

Copyright 2016 J.D. Mallinson

Inspector Mason mysteries:

Danube Stations
The File on John Ormond
The Italy Conspiracy
The Swiss Connection
Quote for a Killer
Death by Dinosaur

CHAPTER 1

It was a fine afternoon in early June when Irina Carmichael left her home close to the center of Christchurch, a medium-sized coastal town in the county of Hampshire. As she strode purposefully towards the railway station, noting on the way familiar landmarks such as the medieval minster, she reflected on the advantages of living in such a pleasant environment. Of moderate size, the town had adequate amenities, low crime and an air of gentility not often found nowadays in major population centers. She had congratulated herself many times on the move she had made some years ago with her husband Geoffrey, an agricultural botanist who had transferred from the ivory tower of a Midlands university research department to field projects on working farms throughout the county of Hampshire, with occasional sorties into neighboring Berkshire and Wiltshire. He had successfully established himself in the area as an independent consultant on plant diseases and crop yields.

Increasing her gait, to be in good time for the 2.37 p.m. express to London, she passed a group of Christ's College juniors about to enter the public library. One of them waved at her, but since they all looked much alike in their traditional striped blazers, it was some moments before she recognized her neighbor's boy, Thomas. She smiled a return greeting, recalling with pleasure how he had once taken her punting with his mother on the River Avon. She had much preferred it to the trip out to sea on the large yacht Thomas's father kept a short distance down the coast, at Mudeford. She had only undertaken the voyage to please Geoffrey, for whom sailing in the Bay of Biscay was the ultimate maritime challenge, in some ways comparable to the roaring forties. Fortunately, it had been a relatively calm day and, despite her misgivings, she had quite enjoyed it in the end.

Relaxing in the spacious compartment – mid-afternoon trains were fortunately seldom crowded – she took out her copy of *The Translator*, a novel by the award-winning Sudanese author, Leila Aboulela. It agreeably occupied, in company with refreshments from the service trolley, most of the eighty-minute journey to the capital, which she reached around four o'clock. Reading a book took her mind off current concerns. Alighting from the train at bustling Paddington Station, she took the Bakerloo Line on the Underground as far as Charing Cross, skirting the southern edge of Trafalgar Square to reach Cockspur Street. It was turned half-four when she reached the editorial offices of *Nocturne*, a monthly music magazine with broad appeal edited by her brother-in-law, Cecil Weeks.

"Irina!" he exclaimed cordially, even though relations between them had of late been something less than the optimum. "What a surprise! In town on business, or for shopping?"

Irina occupied the seat facing the editor's cluttered desk, smoothed her pleated skirt and clasped her hands across her lap.

"Let me be frank, Cecil," she began. "I have not heard from my sister in over a week now. Always, when she has been away from home, she has rung me on Sunday morning, just to check in. I am wondering if you have heard from her recently."

Cecil frowned, laying aside an article he was preparing on the coming series of Promenade Concerts at Royal Albert Hall. He was a rather squat individual, slightly overweight, with fleshy features and dark curly hair starting to thin.

"I am truly sorry to hear that, Irina. Since she moved back to Christchurch last March, to begin our trial separation, she has contacted me about once a month. Certainly not within the last week or so."

"Do you happen to know her current assignment? Although Vera now lives close by, and we meet fairly often socially, she rarely discusses her work with me or with Geoffrey."

"By its very nature, her work must be rather hush-hush. Until, of course, it eventually appears in the press. Initially, I am as much in the dark as you are. Have you made enquiries at *The Sunday Post*?"

"I am on my way there, shortly." She paused and pursed her lips, as she framed a more delicate question.

"Something on your mind, Irina?" he intuitively asked, with a quizzical look.

"To be quite frank again, Cecil, I was wondering if something had occurred between the two of you, recently. I am aware that your relationship has deteriorated to some extent over the past twelve months, which is why she sought a trial separation. When Vera gets upset, she does have a tendency to go incommunicado for a while. But she eventually gets over her pique."

Cecil Weeks raised his squat frame from his swivel-chair, leaned across his desk and protested vehemently.

"Nothing at all of that kind, Irina, I do assure you," he said. "Granted, our relationship has been rather cool, but civil enough on the whole. I am in fact sincerely hoping we can get back together again before the year is out. It has been quite a strain for me, I do not mind admitting, living alone these last few months."

Irina Carmichael mellowed a little on hearing that, giving her brother-in-law a more sympathetic look.

"I can appreciate that, Cecil," she remarked. "It occurred to me that Vera might have gone off to your summer cottage in Wales. I tried ringing her there, but received no reply. I tried voice-mail, which has so far remained unanswered."

The editor, mollified, resumed his seat and took up his typescript again.

"To my certain knowledge," he said, "Vera has not visited Wales recently. The utility company would have contacted me about restoring the power, in the event of the property being occupied. The account is in my sole name. Now, if you will excuse me, Irina, I have an important deadline to meet."

Irina took the hint and rose to leave, threading her way back across Trafalgar Square and along The Strand, to reach the editorial offices of *The Sunday Post* on Fleet Street. The managing editor, Auberon Maclintock, informed her that her sister was, strictly speaking, between assignments, but that would not prevent her from undertaking preliminary research on a new topic of interest, to see if it merited a closer look. Irina Carmichael knew full well that, as an investigative journalist, her sister specialized in exposing scams and corruption in the international art market, having often read the fruits of her efforts in the magazine section of *The Sunday Post*. On leaving the premises, she covered the short distance to the Underground station at Aldwych, emerging at Westminster twenty minutes later to pay a visit to Scotland Yard. She expressed her misgivings to Chief Inspector Bill Harrington, who assigned George mason to the case.

*

The following day, Inspector George Mason presented himself at the offices of *Nocturne* on Cockspur Street. Cecil Weeks received him courteously, offering him a seat.

"Your sister-in-law, Irina Carmichael, called at Metropolitan Police Headquarters yesterday," the detective informed him.

"That would be shortly after she came here to see me," the editor said. "She is very concerned at not hearing from my wife in over a week."

"Is that so unusual?"

"They are very close, Inspector, and have an arrangement to keep in regular contact," the musicologist explained. "That is mainly because my wife travels a lot in connection with her work."

"Your wife is, I believe, an investigative journalist," Mason continued. "Can you expand on that?"

"She specializes in the international art market," the editor said. "Her most recent assignment, for instance, took her to Boston. Before that, she was in Prague."

"Have you seen her since her return?"

Cecil Weeks solemnly shook his head.

"I do not know if Irina mentioned to you that Vera and I are not currently living together. We have, in fact, agreed on a trial separation until the end of the year. She, meanwhile, is renting an apartment at Christchurch, quite close to her sister; while I use an address in Chiswick."

"Have you tried telephone contact?" the detective asked.

"Both Irina and I have tried several times to ring her, without success. Her cellphone must be switched off."

George Mason fell silent for a while, weighing up the figure opposite him. He was well aware that, in missing persons cases, the husband was often a prime suspect. And here was this couple, experiencing marriage difficulties. Cecil Weeks, under the stern gaze of the police inspector, shifted his feet uneasily.

"Coffee, Inspector?" he asked, to ease the tension.

Mason nodded curtly and, as the editor momentarily withdrew to the rear of the premises, his eye fell on an opened credit card statement on the corner of the desk. Weeks soon returned with a small tray bearing two cups of coffee, milk and sugar.

"Can you tell me a little more about Vera's Boston trip?" his visitor asked, adding milk but no sugar to the welcome beverage.

"Her article about it appeared in *The Sunday Post* only last week," the other said. "She reported on the smuggling of artworks into America."

"You are referring to stolen artworks?" the detective pointedly asked.

"Mainly," Weeks replied, "but not exclusively. Money laundering or tax evasion can also be involved. A wealthy individual can, for example, purchase a valuable painting here in London and ship it to some obliging art dealer in America. If the documentation for the shipment values it at less than a hundred dollars, U.S. Customs officials will not trouble to open the consignment at the port of entry, for import duty purposes. The painting can then be sold and the proceeds credited, tax-free, to an off-shore bank account in, say, the Cayman Islands."

"Most interesting," Mason remarked. "And an art thief could do likewise?"

"Without question," the editor replied. "Some art galleries and museums do not overly concern themselves with an art work's provenance, so keen are they to acquire valuable exhibits."

The detective sipped his coffee thoughtfully, declining the offer of digestive biscuits to accompany it.

"Do you think, Mr. Weeks," he then asked, "that such investigative work could place your wife in some danger? I mean, people's feathers could be seriously ruffled by enquires like hers."

Cecil Weeks smiled wryly in agreement, while helping himself to another biscuit.

"That possibility has often occurred to me in the past, Inspector," he replied. "And it certainly cannot be ruled out now. But I do not recall her ever having received threats or nuisance calls in connection with her line of work."

George Mason's eye again fell on the credit card statement.

"Do you and your wife," he asked, "keep your personal affairs entirely separate, while living apart? Bank account, telephone bill, credit card, that sort of thing? "

"Vera has her own bank account and cellphone," came the reply. "But we still have, for the time being, a joint credit card. The statement arrived in this morning's mail, as a matter of fact. I was just checking it before you arrived."

"Would you mind if I glanced at it for a moment?" the detective asked.

"Not in the least, Inspector Mason, if you think it may help," the editor replied, passing across the desk.

Mason sipped his coffee, while examining the recorded entries.

"This looks interesting," he said, indicating a transaction for May 28. "Your wife paid sixty-three pounds to East Coast, the rail company operating services from London to Scotland. For a fare of that amount, Mr. Weeks, it is my guess that she went to Edinburgh, or possibly Aberdeen. I shall check the appropriate fare for each destination at King's Cross terminal."

Cecil Weeks gave his visitor a guarded look of approval.

"You may well be correct, Inspector," he said.

The minute George Mason got back to Scotland Yard, Chief Inspector Bill Harrington called him into his office.

"Irina Carmichael just telephoned from Christchurch, Inspector," he began. "She wants to know of any developments."

"I paid a call on Vera Weeks' husband, Cecil," Mason said. "He seems clean enough, from what I could gather. No reason as yet to suspect him of anything untoward. Although, interestingly enough, the couple are on a trial separation."

"What makes you so sure, Inspector?"

"I just returned from King's Cross, Chief Inspector, using information from the Weeks' joint credit card. Vera Weeks booked a rail ticket to Edinburgh ten days ago, without informing either her sister or her husband. She is an investigative journalist who may be on to something she prefers to remain quiet about for the time being. Her editor at *The Sunday Post*, Auberon Maclintock, is under the impression that she is between journalistic assignments."

"That seems a fairly plausible reading of the situation," Harrington said. "Are you now anticipating a trip to Scotland?"

"I am thinking of going up there tomorrow, on the afternoon train," his colleague replied, "after tying up loose ends here on a recent case. It may also be a good idea to invite Irina Carmichael along."

"With a view that, knowing her sister's habits, she might be of practical assistance?"

"Something on those lines, Sir, yes," George Mason replied.

"Then get in touch with her, by all means, if she is prepared to pay her own expenses. Our department budget will not extend to complimentary highland tours for the general public."

George Mason smiled to himself at his senior's sense of irony. As Harrington's hand hovered near the drawer where he kept his single-malt whisky – he often liked a tot to chase his morning coffee - Mason returned to his own quarters and placed a call to Christchurch.

"Irina Carmichael," came the immediate reply.

"Good morning, Mrs. Carmichael," the detective said. "I hope you are feeling well?"

"Very well, thank you, Inspector Mason, apart from my concern about Vera."

"How does a trip to Scotland strike you?"

"Scotland!" she exclaimed, incredulously.

"Your sister booked a ticket to Edinburgh some days ago. The Chief Inspector and I thought you might wish to accompany me, to see if we can pick up her trail."

There was a pause, during which he assumed she was considering the proposition.

"When do you intend to leave, Inspector?" she enquired, after a few moments.

"Tomorrow afternoon."

"I think I should be able to manage that," she then said, in a tone betraying a certain eagerness. "After I have cleared it with my husband, Geoffrey. Can I call you back?"

"I shall be in the office all day, doing paperwork," he replied. "You can catch me any time before 5.00 p.m."

CHAPTER 2

The following day, Irina Carmichael arrived at King's Cross terminal a little after two o'clock, to meet George Mason in good time to buy tickets for the 2.25 p.m. East Coast service to Edinburgh. She was a tall, slender woman in her early forties, with dark chin-length hair, wearing a brown pleated skirt and loose tan jacket with a Gucci shoulder bag. She carried an overnight valise. The detective spotted her some distance away, as soon after she entered the station concourse, from the brief description she had given the previous day over the telephone.

"Glad you could make it, Irina," he said, as they joined the queue at the booking-office.

"Geoffrey was only too pleased for me to come," she replied. "He thought it would help set my mind at rest, and that a short break would do me good."

"Good thinking," Mason said, eventually leading the way to the Inter-city express standing at Platform 9. They found comfortable seats in a second-class compartment and observed the bustle on the platform before a sharp whistle heralded departure, bang on time.

"Been to Scotland before?" he enquired.

"Several times," Irina replied. "When we were a bit younger, Geoffrey and I used to go skiing in the Cairngorms. We also liked to visit the Trossachs and Loch Lomond."

"A beautiful country," Mason said, with feeling. "I myself have never skied in Scotland, preferring the Dolomites, where the snow-cover is more reliable. It can be patchy in Scotland."

"We once went to Saas Fee, in Switzerland," Irina said. "We have never been to Italy."

"A pleasure in store, I assure you. Tell me a bit about Christchurch."

"It is lovely old town, quite near the sea. Rather old-world in many ways, but we like the civility and neighborliness."

"What exactly do you do there, may I ask?"

"Geoffrey is an agricultural botanist, specializing in plants diseases and crop yields."

"Sounds good," the detective opined. "A useful sort of job."

"My husband loves it, since it keeps him mainly out-of-doors."

"And you yourself?"

"I have a part-time job at the library. In my spare moments, between the garden and the kitchen, I write historical novels."

"You don't say so!" George Mason exclaimed. "How interesting is that!"

"I find it so," she replied. "I majored in history at Sussex University. My writing is sort of an extension of that."

"Any particular period?"

"The Tudor era and the nineteenth century."

"Lots of material there," the detective agreed. "I have always been interested, from a professional point of view, in period murder."

"That is understandable," came the reply.

"In the eighteen hundreds, for example, the most popular means of doing away with someone was arsenic poisoning."

"As in the novels of Agatha Christie?"

"Exactly so," her companion said, rising to his theme. "For one thing, it was very difficult to detect, since the symptoms were similar to those of common stomach ailments. It could also be administered in small doses over time, which is the typical way wives employed it to rid themselves of abusive husbands. The notorious Lafarge case in nineteenth-century Paris provides a good example."

"Fascinating, Inspector," an intrigued Irina Carmichael commented.

"Arsenic was also prescribed medically for a variety of common ailments, such as cramps, asthma and typhus. It was very cheap and widely available at pharmacies. Eventually, a test to trace it in the body was invented and its usage declined."

"I imagine, too, that the advent of laws enabling divorce also contributed to that. Wives would no longer need to eliminate abusive husbands."

George Mason smiled at that observation. It was not something that would have occurred to him.

"Quite probably so," he conceded. "While we are on the subject of spousal murder, what is your view of Cecil Weeks? I mean, have you any reason to believe he might harm your sister?"

Irina Carmichael looked momentarily stunned at that remark.

"I cannot imagine a more remote possibility, Inspector Mason," she replied. "Cecil is fond of my sister. It is Vera, in point of fact, who sought the trial separation."

"On what grounds, may I ask?"

"That is something I would not wish to go into at the moment. I do not really think it has much bearing on the case."

"As you wish," Mason considerately replied.

They passed the remainder of the long journey alternately reading and indulging in sporadic conversation, avoiding for the time being the subject which had brought them together in the first place, Irina's sister Vera. On the way, they noted items of interest, such as York Minster and Durham Cathedral, viewed from the express train.

"The Venerable Bede lies in Durham Cathedral," the detective observed, as the train approached the environs of the imposing structure built on a promontory overlooking a broad river.

"I did not know that," his companion replied. "But I guess it figures. This was his home turf."

"Wasn't he the historian of Anglo-Saxon England, living around 800 A.D.?"

"Indeed he was," Irina replied. "And he was the person who actually first used the tag A.D. – *anno domini* – in his writings. He also instituted a more rigorous historical method."

"You mean in an age when people more often relied on miracles, omens and rank hearsay?"

"Exactly, Inspector," Irina replied. "Written records were not methodically kept until a much later date, so it was hard to sift fact from fiction."

"As it still is today," Mason wryly quipped. "Can we believe everything we read in the newspapers, for example?"

"I guess not," came the good-humored reply.

Around five o'clock, they took light refreshments from the passing trolley. It was well past seven by the time they reached their destination. George Mason hailed a cab outside Waverley Station, directing it to Holloway Hotel on Regent Terrace, where he had pre-booked two rooms. It overlooked the Nelson Monument in Regent Gardens, a stone's throw from the Royal Mile. They located their rooms along the winding corridors of the second floor, deposited their luggage and met up again for a late dinner. Before ordering, Irina Carmichael glanced round at the other tables in the restaurant, in the vain hope of catching sight of her sister, even though a check with Reception revealed that no Vera Weeks had ever stayed at this establishment. After the meal, feeling tired from the long journey, she opted for an early night. George Mason repaired to the bar for a nightcap. After scanning the pages of *The Scotsman* broadsheet, he made plans for the day ahead.

Irina Carmichael, much refreshed, was down early for breakfast, enjoying a cup of fresh coffee while catching the strains of a distant bagpiper. George Mason hove into view twenty minutes later, joining her at a window table in the spacious restaurant, which was almost full.

"Do I hear the sound of bagpipes?" he genially enquired.

"It is near the height of the tourist season, Inspector," his companion replied. "Sounds like it may be coming from the castle precinct."

"That figures," Mason said. "Edinburgh Castle is a major tourist draw. It gets droves of visitors throughout the season."

They studied the menu briefly, opting for traditional Scottish fare of porridge, followed by Loch Fyne kippers.

"Your sister is an investigative journalist, I believe," he began.

Irina nodded, saying:

"She has been concentrating on shadier aspects of the art world, such as the smuggling of stolen paintings and miniature sculptures."

"Beats me how they find a market for their ill-gotten goods," the detective remarked, helping himself to coffee.

"Art galleries, auction houses, dealers and private collectors do not always check the provenance of objects that interest them," Irina said.

"Because they are so keen to acquire them?"

"Exactly, Inspector," she replied, with a knowing smile. "It may seem odd, but anyone can check on stolen art works at the Art Loss Registry in London, which keeps a comprehensive database. Surprisingly, not all buyers take that precautionary step."

"Quite amazing," Mason remarked, as he added milk and sugar to his warm cereal. "What I propose to do this morning – with your agreement, that is – is visit the main art galleries in this city, on the assumption that Vera may have called at one or more of them while in Edinburgh."

"We can make a start straight after breakfast," Irina agreed, nudging the half-eaten bowl of porridge aside to tackle the kippers, carefully removing the bones.

"To save time, we had best split up," the detective suggested. "You could call at the Royal Scottish Academy and National Gallery."

"How do I locate them?" she asked.

"They are both central and, in fact, quite close together. On exiting the hotel, turn left along Market Street and continue past Waverley Station, where we arrived last night, towards The Mound, which is just below Castle Rock. Ask to speak with the curators, if available, or their assistants. They will probably know your sister by reputation, at the very least, in view of her publication record."

"And where shall you be, meanwhile, Inspector Mason?"

"I shall pay a visit to The Dean's Gallery, The Caledonian and the Fruit Market Gallery. That should give us fairly comprehensive coverage of the major art museums."

"We meet up for lunch?"

"Around one o'clock, I suggest, at the station buffet. That will be easy to find, so we don't somehow miss each other."

The matter settled, they concentrated on their tasty food, while still enjoying the strains of the lone bagpiper. George Mason opened the window a bit wider, the better to hear it, reflecting how much more he enjoyed a soloist than the massed bagpipes of, for example, the Edinburgh Military Tattoo. On eventually rising from table, they went their separate ways.

His gaze followed Irina for a few moments as she headed briskly along Market Street towards the castle, before he made his way, with the aid of a street-map, to Belford Road. Twenty minutes later, he was standing inside The Dean's Gallery, admiring its collection of modern art. Even though the likes of Picasso, Salvador Dali and Magritte had never greatly appealed to him, he passed an interesting fifteen minutes, in company with a handful of other art-fanciers, surveying the contents, amazed at their variety and originality. Modern art was nothing if not highly original.

When he finally managed to speak to the curator, he was informed that Vera Weeks had indeed visited the premises a few days ago, showing particular interest in their post-Impressionist paintings. The curator, who had previously had professional dealings with the journalist, had not noticed anything unusual in her demeanor. He had formed the impression that she was currently interested in oriental sculpture, an area he himself was not very well up on.

"What do you mean, precisely, by oriental sculpture?" the detective asked him.

"There is a great deal of interest in Chinese artifacts, in particular," the other explained. "It is a result of the emergence of China as a world trading partner."

"In the sense that it has opened up," George Mason asked, "after decades spent as a very closed society?"

The curator nodded.

"The Cultural Revolution was mainly responsible for that," he explained. "The regime was extremely wary of Western influences. Nowadays, frequent visits by Western businessmen have revived interest in Chinese culture generally."

George Mason thanked the man for that information and retraced his steps towards Market Street and the Fruit Market Gallery, which also specialized in contemporary art. The resident staff had not, however, met recently with Vera Weeks, although they were familiar with her investigations into less edifying aspects of the international art market. He had better luck at The Caledonian, in the Canongate area of the city. The curator, Sir Archer Tate, received him in his private office and bade him take a seat, while answering the telephone. Mason glanced at the pictures mounted on the walls. They were more to his personal taste, being mainly scenes of the Highlands, wildlife and the Scottish coast. His wife Adele, on the other hand, professed strong interest in abstract art; she would have loved it, he mused, at the two previous galleries he had visited. A glance at his watch told him it was almost eleven; he had plenty of time before meeting Irina.

"What can I do for you, Inspector Mason?" Sir Archer enquired, on replacing the receiver.

"I am trying to trace an investigative journalist named Vera Weeks," the detective replied. "We know for a fact that she recently came to Edinburgh. I am wondering if she visited this gallery at any time."

"She was here just three days ago," came the prompt reply. "Is everything all right?"

"She has not been in touch with her family," Mason explained. "Her sister Irina has grown concerned about her. We are both here making routine enquiries, in case the nature of her work has aroused enmity in some quarters."

"The art mafia, perhaps?"

"We have no leads, so far," his visitor explained. "Did you meet with her personally at this address?"

"Indeed I did, Inspector Mason. And it was an eye-opener for me."

"What precisely do you mean by that, Sir Archer?"

"Vera informed me that a painting in our collection was a forgery."

"Which item would that be?" the intrigued detective asked.

"Vermeer's *Girl Writing a Letter*."

"Vermeer being the Dutch painter of mainly domestic scenes?" George Mason asked.

"Spot on, Inspector!" came the reply. "You evidently know your old masters. Vermeer lived in seventeenth-century Delft. Vera also informed me that three other important galleries, one in Poland and two in Austria, claim to have the same painting."

George Mason's brow puckered.

"You are referring to forgeries?" he enquired, in puzzlement.

"One of them, of course, will be the authentic canvas," the curator replied. "Many art galleries and museums hold fakes they are not even aware of. Forgers are highly-skilled people, skilled artists in their own right, as a matter of fact. For example, they will execute a painting in the style of an old master, say from the Renaissance, and claim that it is a hitherto undiscovered work that only recently came to light."

"The way valuables sometimes turn up in someone's basement or attic?"

"Correct again, Inspector."

"But how are the galleries so easily duped?" Mason wanted to know.

"Often enough," came the reply, "they just look at the general style and the signature. If it seems authentic, they will often accept it, in their eagerness to own a previously unknown masterpiece."

"You amaze me, Sir Archer."

The curator smiled and raised his arms in mock despair.

"So how did Vera Weeks decide that your copy was a fake?" his visitor then asked.

"She brought in an expert from Stirling University," Tate replied, "after learning that one of the examples in Vienna was also declared a fake. Artists in different periods – the Rococo, say, or the Baroque – used the pigments then available to them. Each pigment reacts differently to the ageing process. A forger can only use modern pigments, which an expert can readily identify. Additionally, the odor of linseed oil dissipates over time. If it is still evident on a canvas, then the painting must be of recent origin."

"Quite remarkable!" the detective exclaimed. "What, in your view, is the motive behind the forgeries? Is it simply to make money?"

"That is only one explanation of their dubious activities," Tate explained, "though doubtless a valid one. Some, on the other hand, take satisfaction from the mere fact of duping the art establishment."

"You mean," Mason said, "that they develop some sort of animus against the art world?"

"They may well do so," came the reply, "especially if they feel that their own worth is not sufficiently recognized. Or they may simply wish to cock a snook at the art world, regarding it as over-pompous and pretentious."

"Did Vera Weeks give you any idea of what her plans were after leaving these premises?" the detective then asked.

"She informed me that she had long harbored suspicions about one of our Scottish artists named Rory MacTaggart, but that her other commitments – she was recently in America, I believe – prevented her from pursuing them. She is now in-between journalistic assignments, I believe, and may decide to devote some time to this project. It would be of considerable interest to us if she can pin a forgery on him."

"What is your own opinion of this Rory MacTaggart, Sir Archer?"

"I have never met him personally," came the reply. "But I know of him as an accomplished painter of Hebridean landscapes, who has not so far held a major exhibition of his work."

"Residing here in Edinburgh?"

The curator smilingly shook his head.

"About as far away as one can get from the art establishment," he replied. "MacTaggart lives in Tobermory."

"On the Isle of Mull?" an intrigued George Mason asked.

Archer Tate nodded.

"Vera Weeks had it in mind to pay him a visit," he said, "but I do not know if she followed through on that."

"It would be worth looking into, though," his visitor said. "Thank you very much, Sir Archer, for your time and for your helpful information."

"Do not mention it, Inspector Mason. I am at your disposal any time."

With that, Mason left The Caledonian and headed back across George 1V Bridge towards Market Street, musing the while on the interesting facts the curator had told him. Being a little early for his reunion with Irina, he dropped by The Castle pub for a quick half-pint of ale, before entering Waverley Station. By the time he reached the buffet, she was already ensconced at a corner table, sipping lemon-tea while reading a magazine.

"I have been here about ten minutes," she explained, on rising to greet him. "Thought I would wait until you arrived before ordering food."

"What are they offering?" he enquired, sitting opposite her.

"The usual station buffet fare. I have already decided on a prawn open sandwich."

George Mason quickly scanned the menu.

"I think I shall settle for cheese-on-toast," he said "I am not all that hungry after a full breakfast."

They placed their order, to include a pot of orange pekoe tea, and sat back to watch the bustle on Market Street through the buffet window.

"Any luck this morning?" he enquired.

"I visited the galleries you mentioned on The Mound," Irina replied. "Vera had been to both quite recently."

"And?"

"I got to speak with the assistant curator each time. My sister was apparently interested in their most recent acquisitions, mainly Post-Impressionist."

"Such as Seurat, Cezanne and van Gogh?"

Irina nodded, inwardly impressed that a policeman was conversant with modern art.

"Was the question of forgeries raised?" he asked.

"Not in my presence," Irina replied. "Galleries are not generally willing to admit the possibility that they may own fakes. Their reputation is at stake."

At that moment, their simple meal arrived, occupying their attention.

"The issue cropped up at The Caledonian," George Mason said, after a while. "Vera Weeks and an expert from Stirling University decided that one of their Vermeers was a fake. What is more, the curator claimed that Vera suspected who the forger was, and that she had had him in her sights for some time."

"Vera never lets go when she thinks she is on to something," Irina said, emphatically. "Investigative work like that is her bread-and-butter. Exposing a fraud would greatly enhance her reputation in art circles."

George Mason gave a wry smile, while finishing his Welsh rarebit.

"You know your sister very well," he remarked. "Sir Archer Tate, the Caledonian curator, suggested she may have gone to Tobermory."

"The Isle of Mull!" the other exclaimed, almost choking on her prawn sandwich.

"That's where the suspected forger, Rory MacTaggart, has his studio."

Irina Carmichael took a sip of hot tea and fixed her companion with a curiously quizzical look. Mason merely returned an ironic smile, waiting for her to come to terms with the obvious, which she did, with an air of reluctance.

"We shall have to go there," she solemnly announced.

"It is a fair hop from Edinburgh," he said. "Sure you are up for it?"

"It is not as if we have many other leads, Inspector," she replied, with a hint of exasperation. "How soon could we be there?"

"You sit right here, Irina, and finish your snack, while I go make enquiries at the Information Desk."

With that, he drained his lukewarm tea, left the buffet and headed briskly across the main concourse, dodging the stream of passengers newly alighting from the Glasgow express. Joining the short queue, he patiently waited his turn, returning to the buffet some twenty minutes later.

"There is a train to Oban leaving in just under an hour," he informed her. "After an overnight stay there, we can catch the morning ferry to the Isle of Mull."

"Which gives us just enough time to return to Holloway Hotel and retrieve our luggage," Irina said.

"Then let us do that," he agreed.

CHAPTER 3

After calling briefly at Glasgow, their train headed north-west towards the coast, through some of the most scenic parts of the Highlands. Irina Carmichael resumed reading the *The Translator*, which she had not had an opportunity to open since her trip to London. Its compelling narrative, which had a strong Scottish interest, helped take her mind off current concerns. George Mason contented himself with enjoying the scenery, reminding himself of a skiing holiday he had enjoyed with friends at Glencoe years ago in his bachelor days. Conditions had been rather icy, he recalled, causing frequent falls; a far cry from the powder snow prevalent in the Alps. He had counted himself lucky not to sustain serious injury. When the refreshment trolley rolled by, his companion laid her half-finished book aside as they both bought soft drinks.

"When is the train due in, Inspector?" Irina Carmichael enquired.

"Early evening, assuming no delays," the detective replied.

"We could look for accommodation down by the harbor, to save time tomorrow morning," she suggested.

"Probably a good idea," he agreed. "I doubt we shall have trouble finding somewhere, even near the height of the tourist season. There is a lot of choice. They practically live from tourism in towns like Oban, it being the main point of departure for the Hebrides."

"Edinburgh was full of visitors already," Irina remarked. "Especially in the castle precinct."

"Did you visit it yourself?"

"I had a half-hour to spare after calling at the art galleries. Enough to view the courtyard, the battlements and pay a short visit to the souvenir shop."

"I gather it has a rather violent history," her companion remarked.

"You can say that again, Inspector. It changed hands quite often between the English and the Scots, during wars for Scottish independence. It was also a focus of conflict among the various clans, in the period following independence. Two young Scottish princes were executed there, by a rival claimant to the throne."

"Much like the princes in the Tower of London?" Mason put in.

Irina, a historical novelist, nodded agreement.

"I prefer to think of the castle in its modern role, as backdrop to the annual Military Tattoo," she said.

"Floodlighting, kilts, bagpipes?"

"I was up here once for the Edinburgh Festival, at a symposium on young-adult fiction. That is the only time I have watched the Tattoo live."

"Quite an experience, I imagine," the detective duly considered. "I have only ever watched it on television."

Irina smiled, a trifle archly, at that remark and took up her reading again. George Mason rose from his seat and made his way down the train to the buffet car for a beer, to help pass the remainder of the journey. The train, subject to a delay caused by a signal fault, arrived twenty minutes behind schedule. The pair quickly made their way down to the harbor, where they experienced little difficulty booking rooms at Trossachs Inn. The following morning, after an early breakfast, they caught the ferry to Craignure, a bracing hour-long voyage across the Firth of Lorn, accompanied by seagulls and some larger birds Mason thought might be gannets. Duarte Castle, seat of Clan McLean, loomed on the skyline. From the port of entry, it was a short bus drive to Tobermory. George Mason had looked up MacTaggart's address in the Mull telephone directory after his late dinner in Oban.

On alighting from the bus, they approached an elderly man sitting on the quayside gazing out across the Sound of Mull towards the mist-shrouded hills of Argyll.

"Could you possibly direct us to Back Brae?" the detective asked.

The man turned and carefully appraised the visitors. With a twinkle in his eye, he said:

"Ye'd be lookin' for the artist Rory MacTaggart," he said, "I have nae doubt?"

"That is correct," Mason smilingly replied, with an amused glance at his companion.

"Proceed along Breadalbane Street and take a right onto Jubilee Terrace. Back Brae's the first turn left after that. That's where ye'll find him, if he's at home. Spends a lot of time fishin' out on the bay. I've been sittin' here a wee while, but I havena spotted his boat. Ye may be in luck."

Mason thanked him as the pair set off on a narrow road leading up from the quay. Minutes later, they were standing outside 6 Back Brae, a stone cottage partly covered with ivy. Mason struck the heavy brass knocker. Moments later, the door opened, to reveal a well-built man with a ruddy complexion beneath tousled hair, clad in a paint-daubed smock. The detective estimated him to be in his late forties.

"Good day," the man said, carefully scrutinizing the pair. "What can I do for ye?"

George Mason showed ID.

"We are making enquiries about a missing journalist named Vera Weeks," he began.

MacTaggart's face darkened momentarily, before a wry smile crossed his sea-weathered features.

"Ye had both better step inside," he said, opening the front door wider to admit them to a living-room furnished in rustic style. Adjoining that was a larger, open area with easels, some of which were mounted with canvases. They were invited to sit on hard chairs facing a bare pinewood table.

"We understand that Vera Weeks may have paid you a visit recently," Mason said.

"She did indeed, Sir," the other cagily replied.

"What day would that be?" Irina Carmichael asked.

"Three days ago, on June 10," came the prompt reply.

"What was the reason for her visit?" the detective asked.

MacTaggart pursed his lips and grimaced.

"She had this preposterous notion that I forged a painting by Vermeer, currently on view at The Caledonian in Edinburgh."

"Would that be *Girl Writing a Letter*?"

"The very same," came the surprised reaction.

"And you deny it is a forgery?"

"Absolutely. I am respected artist in my own right. I do local views and seascapes. Take a look round my studio and see for yerselves."

"I shall take your word for it, Mr. MacTaggart." Mason said. "Sir Archer Tate apprised me of your status as a landscape painter."

"The Weeks woman was prying into things," the artist continued, "to boost her standing as a journalist. A regular busy-body, if ever there was one."

"Did she threaten to expose you for forgery?" Irina asked.

"You're darned right she did. In *The Sunday Post* too, just to please the highbrows in London. I thought at first that she had come all this way to interview me about my work, with a view to my getting wider recognition. I showed her my studio and recent canvases, made her a cup of tea with a dram of whisky and discussed Scottish art. When, after an hour or so, she gingerly mentioned the Vermeer, I soon showed her the door."

There was silence, as the visitors absorbed that information. Since they said nothing, the light of understanding slowly dawned across the Scot's shrewd features. With an ironic smile, he said:

"Ye are here because you think I may have harmed her."

"You might have a motive," the detective suggested.

The artist's heavy frame shook with laughter. Composing himself, he said:

"Ye'll ne'er pin something like that on me, Inspector Mason. She left Tobermory the very same day she arrived. I checked with MacBride, who runs the local taxi service. He drove her to Craignure, where she caught the late ferry back to Oban. Check with him for yerself. His rank is on Argyll Terrace."

George Mason and Irina Carmichael glanced at each other uncertainly.

"Tell me, Mr. MacTaggart," the detective said, "how you would account for the fake Vermeer at The Caledonian."

"Most art galleries have their share of fakes," came the reply. "Also of stolen paintings. They get them through unscrupulous dealers."

"Who acquire them from thieves and forgers?"

The artist nodded disingenuously, before adding:

"I'm sorry if ye feel ye have wasted yer valuable time."

"These are just routine enquiries, Mr. MacTaggart, at this stage," Mason explained. "If we decide to take the matter further, the local police will be involved."

The Scot mockingly dismissed the idea.

"They will find nothing to interest them here," he assured them.

"It has, in fact, been quite a useful visit," Irina put in, "in that we now know for sure that my sister was here in Tobermory just three days ago. We have no reason, as yet, to think she may have come to any harm."

"I shall gladly make ye both a cup of tea," a more mollified Rory MacTaggart offered.

"That will not be necessary," the detective said, rising to his feet. "But thanks for your kind offer all the same."

"Do not take much notice of what ye may read in *The Sunday Post*," he said, as a parting shot, as the visitors stepped outside. "*The Scottish Independent* is more reliable."

George Mason returned an amused smile at that remark and bade the man good day. The visitors then headed back down Breadalbane Street towards the quay. Mainly as a matter of courtesy, they called at the local police station. Sergeant Diarmid MacNiece, the officer-in-charge, was much surprised by their appearance.

"Scotland Yard up here in the Inner Hebrides?" he queried.

George Mason explained their errand, enquiring if the local police had noticed anything unusual in the past few days.

"We have had our share of tourists, that's for sure," MacNiece informed them. "One of them, a Japanese visitor, comes to mind."

"Why would that be?" Mason asked.

"Japanese, and also the Chinese visitors we are seeing more of nowadays, invariably arrive in groups. They may be small family groups or large parties coming by coach from the mainland. This particular visitor seemed to be very much on his own. In a village like this, individuals tend to stand out."

"Did he act in such a way as to arouse suspicion?" George Mason immediately asked.

"My constable, Hugh Douglas, kept an eye on him, from time to time. The person in question did not do typical tourist activities, like sailing, bird-watching, visiting the museum and the art galleries. He just seemed to hang around for a day or two, mainly along the quayside, with occasional visits to the Macdonald Arms."

"That is rather curious," Mason agreed. "Did you or your constable also notice an Englishwoman here three days ago?" He was wondering if there might possibly be a connection between the two.

The sergeant emphatically shook his head.

"Do you have a description of the man?" Irina asked.

"They all look the same to me," came the reply. "Constable Douglas thought he was a youngish man, perhaps a college student. That is about all I can tell you."

"Thanks all the same for your help, Sergeant MacNiece," Mason said, as the pair left the station and made their way along Main Street. It was now mid-afternoon and they had eaten nothing since their breakfast.

"I suggest we call at Macdonald Arms," he said, "and grab a bite to eat. After that, we shall take a taxi to Craignure in good time to catch the evening ferry back to Oban."

"I shall second that, Inspector," Irina Carmichael said. "I am quite peckish, as a matter of fact, after all this trailing around."

"I expect the pub will serve typical Scottish fare," George Mason said.

"So long as it is not haggis," his companion half-seriously replied.

On reaching the quayside, they spent a few minutes admiring the colorful waterfront buildings of the old fishing port and watching the boats bobbing at anchor on the bay, wondering which one belonged to the artist. The elderly gentleman was still sitting there, gazing out to sea. George Mason took him to be a retired mariner or fisherman. A short walk brought them to the pub. Once inside, they occupied stools at the bar and ordered drinks, finding themselves in the interval between lunch and evening meal service. They had to make do with left-over pickled herring sandwiches, while promising to do justice to a three-course hotel dinner later on. Trossachs Inn had a very good table.

Mid-afternoon trade being slack, the barman was talkative.

"What brings ye both to the Hebrides?" he asked, serving them glasses of lager.

"Routine business," Mason replied, non-commitally.

"Ye are not tourists then?"

Irina firmly shook her head.

"I could readily spend a vacation here," she remarked. "It is a very appealing place."

"And quite popular, too, considering its remoteness," the barman said. "Visitors who come this far often go on, to Staffa and Iona, reached by boat from the west coast of Mull."

"Fingal's Cave?" Mason enquired, thinking of the orchestral piece by Felix Mendelssohn.

The barman smiled appreciatively at his knowledge of music.

"Ye might also sight the white-tailed eagle," he continued, "which has lately begun to breed again in these parts."

"Wildlife is staging quite a come-back all across Europe," Irina Carmichael knowledgeably remarked. "Ibis and chamois in the Alps. Wild boars in England, France and Italy. Wolves, elks and lynx farther east."

"Whereas in England we make do with badgers, foxes and otters," Mason ironically observed.

"We have too many wild cats in Scotland," the barman complained. "They are so numerous experts have difficulty identifying the original native species, as distinct from those cross-bred with feral cats."

Having said that, he moved farther down the bar to serve another customer, leaving the visitors to their simple meal.

*

Several hours later, after a calm crossing, the visitors took their places in the dining-room of Trossachs Inn, listening to the ceilidh in full swing in the adjoining bar. Scanning the menu, they both opted for Dover sole with jacket potatoes and a half-carafe of New Zealand Chardonnay. A young waitress, traditionally dressed in a tartan skirt and cream-colored blouse, took their order, returning within minutes to serve the chilled wine.

"What was your impression of Rory MacTaggart?" the detective asked his companion, soon as he had approved the wine.

"I thought he was patently insincere," Irina replied "regarding the Vermeer canvas. If, as you were informed, there are at least three other forgeries of the same painting, it is a safe bet that Vera was on the right track. She is meticulously careful about her investigative sources."

"If MacTaggart has a sideline in forged paintings, that is not really our concern," Mason said. "It is something for the Argyll Constabulary to look into. We can be reasonably sure your sister left Mull in good health. I am inclined towards thinking she has gone incommunicado, for whatever reason, rather than missing, in the strict sense of that word."

Irina weighed his remarks carefully for a few moments.

"This is so unlike her," she said, sipping her wine. "Wherever she is now, she is just three days ahead of us. If we can somehow trace her movements from June 10 ..."

"...we shall be home and dry," Mason added.

Their welcome meal being served, they concentrated on food for a while, as the sound of the entertainment spilled over from the adjoining bar, which was crowded with mainly-young Obanites. The ceilidh, the waitress explained, took place every Friday evening and sometimes on national holidays as well. Irina, particularly, loved the spontaneous Gaelic music; it helped soothe her feelings of anxiety. She sat back in her chair to enjoy it to the full.

George Mason, on finishing his appetizing meal, ordered coffee and a tot of single malt from the local distillery. Irina Carmichael, with good appetite after their long day, promptly ordered fig pudding for dessert, declining her companion's offer of a Gaelic coffee.

"One possible way to trace Vera's movements," the detective suggested, as the waitress eventually cleared their empty plates, "would be to check transactions on her credit card."

"Vera rarely uses credit," Irina countered. "She generally prefers cash or check."

"Worth a try, though," Mason persisted. "After dinner, I shall give Cecil Weeks a call. Since they still - rather surprisingly, to my mind - have a joint credit account, he should be able to check, with a straightforward telephone call, any expenses recently charged to it."

Irina smiled at his acumen and nodded in agreement.

"Worth a try, certainly, Inspector," she said, giving him her brother-in-law's home telephone number.

Leaving his companion to enjoy the folk music, the detective rose from his place and went to the booth in the lobby. Since the facility was in use, he stepped outside momentarily to get a breath of fresh air and watch the lights of what he took to be fishing boats out on the firth. On finally accessing the booth, he found Cecil Weeks at home, chatted briefly with him and requested that he ring the credit card company. The musicologist agreed to do so and promised to ring back. Mason hovered in the reception area, allowing Weeks twenty minutes to complete his enquiries and get back to him.

"My hunch was correct," he informed Irina, on eventually returning to the table.

"Vera has used her card?" she asked, in surprise.

"She made two transactions on June 11," he announced. "The first was at a car-hire firm in Glasgow. The second was at Arklet Studio, Inversnaid."

"June 11 would be the day after she left Mull," Irina figured, on quick reflection. "But where on earth is Inversnaid?"

"It is a village on the east bank of Loch Lomond," the detective said.

"We should go there, in that case, without delay."

"We can hardly get to Inversnaid this evening," he replied. "It is way up in the Highlands. What I suggest is that we take the train back to Glasgow first thing after breakfast tomorrow morning. Once there, we can hire a car for the drive north. It should not take too long."

"Sounds good," a more relaxed Irina said. "I would be curious to discover what, if anything, she bought at the studio. My sister has often picked up an odd interesting piece of modern art when the opportunity arose."

"It should throw some light on her motives and activities," George Mason said. "Cecil Weeks also told me that Auberon Maclintock at *The Sunday Post* had recently informed him that Vera was observed leaving the Russian Embassy on Kensington Palace Gardens about two weeks ago."

"You don't say so!" Irina exclaimed. "Whatever could she be doing there, I wonder?"

"Anybody's guess," the detective replied. "She could, for example, have applied for a visa."

"To visit Russia?" an incredulous Irina asked. "If she had such a thing in mind, she never mentioned it to me."

"There seems to be quite a secretive side to your sister's life," he pointedly observed.

"You can say that again," the other remarked. "The Russian Embassy, for heaven's sake! I do hope it was for something as simple and straightforward as a travel visa."

"She may have a professional interest in Russian art," Mason suggested.

"That is also possible," Irina agreed.

They fell silent for a while, each engrossed in his own thoughts.

"What I propose now," George Mason said, after a while, "is that we transfer to the adjoining bar and enjoy the rest of the ceilidh. I could then use a good night's sleep."

"Here, here!" his companion eagerly rejoined. "It has been a very full day. But what a stroke of luck we should have stayed at this inn on the very night they have live music! It so takes one's mind, even if temporarily, off current problems."

*

The following day, they proceeded as planned, arriving at Glasgow Central around mid-morning. Hiring a Peugeot sedan from Rent-a-Car, they soon reached the west bank of Loch Lomond, enjoying a scenic drive as far as Invergulas. They parked the car there and took the ferry across to Inversnaid. A fellow-passenger pointed out a cave on the opposite bank, visible only from the lake, saying that it was one of Rob Roy MacGregor's hideouts.

"Quite fascinating," George Mason observed. "I understand that he managed to evade capture by English troops and died peacefully in bed, of old age."

"He began life as a respected cattle dealer," Irina added, "but he had difficulty repaying loans made by wealthy lairds, who then seized his estates, depriving him of a livelihood."

"So he became a cattle rustler in revenge?"

"Also a kind of Robin Hood, giving aid to the poor."

"The Duke of Argyll sheltered him at critical times," their fellow-passenger said. "The Highlands were even wilder then than they are now, with poor communications and plenty of cover."

"His status as Scottish folk hero seems assured," George Mason pointedly observed, "despite some questionable activities."

"A typical lawman's point of view," his companion humorously rejoined.

On disembarking, they walked up to the center of the village, dominated by Inversnaid Hotel. A short distance beyond it, they located Arklet Studio, apparently named after the nearby falls, an impressive cascade of water coursing down from the head of the village to the broad expanse of the loch. On entering, they were cordially greeted by a middle-aged Scotswoman at the service counter. At the sight of the detective's ID, her friendly smile waned into a look of concern.

"What can I do for ye, Inspector?" she enquired, stepping from behind the counter.

"We believe that an Englishwoman we are trying to trace visited your studio three days ago and made a purchase with her credit card, in the sum of seventy-five pounds. This is her sister, Irina, by the way."

"How d'ye do, ma'am," the proprietor said. "I do in fact recall such a person, somewhat resembling your good self. A wee bit older than you, perhaps?"

Irina smiled broadly and said: "Vera Weeks is indeed my elder sister. Would you mind telling us what she purchased here?"

"Using a credit card, she bought a small watercolor by a local artist," the woman replied. "It was not very valuable, but it seemed to appeal to her, perhaps as a memento of her visit to the Highlands. It was a view looking northwards from the loch, towards the Cairngorms."

"How was her general demeanor?" Irina then asked. "I mean, did she seem stressed or harassed in any way?"

The proprietor mused awhile over that question, before answering a telephone call from a prospective customer.

"I would say she seemed preoccupied," she said, at length. "Not so much stressed as serious, business-like. Which is nae surprise, in view of the next purchase she made."

"And what would that be?" an immediately interested George Mason enquired.

"We had a Chinese sculpture on display. A dog's head, executed in bronze, which at once drew her close attention. She appraised it carefully, saying she was very interested but needed to make certain financial arrangements beforehand. She then left these premises - I presume to call her bank manager, or some similar person - and returned about two hours later to complete the purchase. She also mentioned having taken lunch meanwhile at Falls Café, higher up the village."

"She paid for the sculpture by check?" the detective asked.

The proprietor nodded.

"I expect it was quite a valuable piece," Irina Carmichael said.

"Two hundred thousand pounds was the asking price," the other said. "On completing the sale, my assistant crated it for her and placed it in the trunk of her car. It occurred to me that she intended to ship it on."

George Mason whistled aloud. His companion merely looked astonished at that surprising information.

"Is there anything else at all, ma'am, that you can recall about my sister's recent visit?" Irina Carmichael then asked.

"On depositing the crate in her car," came the reply, "my assistant noticed a second car parked directly behind your sister's. It drove off in the same direction immediately after your sister left."

"Does your assistant have any recollection of the driver of the second car?" Mason asked.

"He did mention at the time that the driver looked Asian. You could have asked Donald yerself, but it is his day off and he's off to visit his mother in Dundee. We thought nothing more of it, to tell ye the truth."

The detective thanked the woman for her ready co-operation, as the visitors then briefly admired the finely-crafted contents of the studio before taking their leave. Once outside, since it was well past noon, they made their way higher up the village to Falls Café for a bite to eat.

"Where on earth would Vera obtain such a large sum of money at short notice?" Irina wondered aloud, as they occupied a table overlooking the falls.

George Mason glanced up from the menu and said:

"Perhaps the studio proprietor's surmise was correct, that Vera made arrangements with her bank."

"I still cannot imagine how my sister could summon that amount of money so quickly. She invests the bulk of her savings in pension funds, I do know that, generally keeping fairly modest amounts on deposit, for emergency purposes."

"The plot thickens," her companion said, ordering a bowl of Scotch broth with whole-meal bread. Irina, in turn, opted for an Angus beef sandwich, with horse radish.

"What would Vera want with a Chinese effigy of a dog's head?" Irina also wondered, half-way through her tasty snack. "I could understand her buying a modern painting, but she has never intimated to me any particular interest in sculpture."

"Perhaps she is branching out," Mason suggested. "Expanding her field."

Irina emphatically shook her head.

"No," she replied. "This looks so out of character to me. Not Vera's line of country at all, especially since she has generally limited herself to European art works. Her view of Oriental art was that a fair amount of it was fake."

"That is an interesting viewpoint," the detective said, blowing on his broth to cool it. "I imagine she would have no problem distinguishing the genuine article from a forgery."

They completed their meal in silence, taking in the exhilarating view from the café window. Over coffee afterwards, Irina said:

"What about the person parked behind her at Arklet Studio?"

"You mean, was that person tailing your sister?"

Irina nodded, uneasily.

"Could be just coincidence," Mason said. "There are scores of Asian tourists in Scotland just now."

"Sergeant MacNiece mentioned a young Japanese hanging around Tobermory. What if it was the same person?"

George Mason shrugged.

"It may, or may not, have been," he cagily replied. "There is not much we can do about that now, three days later. But at least we are building up a picture of your sister's movements and activities over the past few days. After lunch, we could take a brief look round the village before returning to Glasgow for an overnight stay. First thing tomorrow morning, I shall ring Chief Inspector Harrington."

The friendly waitress, on overhearing the conversation, said:

"Take a peek inside Inversnaid Hotel, afore ye leave. Queen Victoria herself once stayed there."

"On her way to Balmoral?" an intrigued Irina asked.

"Nae doubt," came the prompt reply. "She loved the Highlands."

"I imagine other famous guests visited this beautiful spot?" George Mason remarked.

"Aye, that's right," came the eager reply. "Sir Walter Scott, our best-known author after Robbie Burns, stayed here while researching his novel *Rob Roy*."

"I shall make a point of reading it," Irina Carmichael said, "knowing something of the background."

CHAPTER 4

Akira Issiguru alighted from a Nippon Airlines overnight flight from Tokyo to Heathrow Airport, passed through Customs and took a taxi to the Japanese Cultural Mission based at Canary Wharf on the River Thames. The journey was slow, on account of the heavy commuter traffic, allowing him the opportunity to reminisce on previous visits to Britain. Two decades ago, he had done post-graduate work in international relations at London School of Economics, earning himself a master's degree. In the intervening years, he had made several visits, mainly of a private nature, to the British capital and surrounding countryside. He had a good command of the language and familiarity with local customs, whose eccentricity invariably intrigued him. It was with a feeling of self-satisfaction that he found himself once again in the United Kingdom, on an assignment of national importance, only the barest details of which had been outlined to him in Tokyo. He was greeted on arrival at Canary Wharf by the head of the mission, Matsuo Yamoto, with whom he had worked years ago on cultural issues in Japan.

"Delighted to meet you again, Akira," Yamoto said, inviting the visitor into his sparsely-furnished office. "How have you been keeping since we last drank sake at Golden Gai?"

"Never better, Matsuo," Issiguru replied.

"And the children?"

"Growing up too fast. Daichi is already at university, studying microbiology. My daughter Chie has just enrolled in high school."

"And Fuji?"

"My wife is keeping well and has recently returned to work, as a cosmetician."

Yamoto solemnly shook his head, indicating mock-disapproval.

"Is it acceptable now in modern Japan," he asked, "for a wife and mother to seek regular paid employment?"

His visitor returned a wry smile.

"I can see, Matsuo, that it is some time since you last visited there. Times are changing, perhaps too rapidly. Japanese women are becoming more independent, many of them preferring careers to marriage and a family. There is no longer any stigma regarding working wives, except perhaps in the most conservative circles."

"I shall take your word for it, Akira," the mission head said. "As a confirmed bachelor myself, I am not really in a position to comment."

With that, he bowed deferentially to his visitor, invited him to sit and bade a young assistant serve tea. Courtesies completed, they got down to business.

"You are aware, of course, Akira, of the reason you were posted here?"

"The briefest of details," the other replied. "The Intelligence Bureau in Tokyo mentioned something about a Chinese sculpture, saying you yourself would fill in the background for me."

Matsuo Yamoto sipped his tea thoughtfully and said: "You are familiar, I take it, with the Boxer Rebellion?"

Akira Issiguru returned a look of considerable surprise.

"Wasn't that something to do with the Opium Wars, if I remember my school history aright?" he tentatively asked.

"Correct, Akira. The Boxers were a secret society dedicated to countering Western influences in China during the late-nineteenth century. Christian missions were among the institutions under attack. Foreign diplomatic staffs were forced to seek refuge in their embassies. The empress herself was quite sympathetic to the movement."

"I recall now, Matsuo, that the Boxers considered themselves invulnerable to bullets, much like the Sioux Indians who died at Wounded Knee."

"You know your American history very well too, honorable friend."

"And wasn't it so, that Western troops arrived to suppress the rebellion?"

"Also correct, Akira. Contingents of troops came from several European countries, led by the British and the French. In the course of the hostilities, the Imperial Summer Palace at Beijing was sacked and its art treasures looted."

"Including a certain bronze sculpture?"

Yamoto gravely nodded.

"It forms part of a group of twelve sculptures representing the Chinese Zodiac that were designed as fountain heads in the courtyard of the imperial summer palace. Each one represents a unique animal."

"Are all of the bronzes missing?" an alert Issiguru asked.

"By no means," came the reply. "The Chinese have recovered a fair number of them and are very keen to complete the set. Trouble is, no one knows where the missing ones are. There is a rumor abroad, however, that one of them, interestingly enough, has recently surfaced in Britain."

"Which is where I come into the picture?" his visitor guardedly enquired.

"Your background in the intelligence service and your knowledge of this country, Akira, make you the obvious person to try and locate it. Assuming, of course, that the rumor is correct. If it is false, you will have an expenses-paid trip to a country which I know you are very fond of, following your time at the university here."

Akira Issiguru slowly sipped his tea, assessing the situation.

"Why is it so important for us to locate it, Matsuo?" he at length enquired.

"The short answer, my friend, is to beat the French to it. There may well be other interested parties, too, but for the time being, we should focus mainly on the French."

"How so, Matsuo?"

The mission head carefully refilled their cups from the elegant china pot and briefly consulted his notes, before saying:

"The French have recently returned two of the Zodiac bronzes, namely the rabbit and the rat, to China, as a gesture of goodwill. Their motivation is to strengthen diplomatic ties after angering the Chinese by official contacts with the Dalai Lama. They are also interested in furthering trade with China, particularly in their luxury goods much sought after by newly-prosperous Chinese consumers. If they can return a third sculpture, it will greatly enhance their standing with the Chinese."

"And it is in our interest to prevent that, Matsuo?" his visitor enquired.

"I have no knowledge, to date, of French intentions in this matter. They may not even be aware that a bronze has resurfaced. But we cannot take that for granted. The Directorate in Paris has very considerable resources at its disposal. If we can locate it first, Akira, that will give us a very strong card to play with our powerful neighbor. When the dispute over sovereignty of the Siriaku Islands is finally resolved, it will greatly improve our relationship with the Chinese if we, rather than the French, can return the bronze."

Akira Issiguru savored his second cup of tea, taking time to absorb his friend's line of reasoning.

"The return of the missing fountain heads must mean a great deal to the Chinese rulers," he eventually remarked.

"It is a question of national pride," the other said. "The looting of art treasures from the Summer Palace was, at the time, a source of acute humiliation for the Chinese. In fact, it still rankles with them."

"So what steps have you taken so far, to identify and locate the supposedly resurfaced bronze?"

"We have recruited a small team of Japanese students on summer vacation from British universities, to help provide leads."

"A rather amateurish approach, Matsuo, don't you consider?" the special agent objected.

The mission head leaned forward across his desk, to emphasize his point.

"For one thing, Akira," he replied, with an artful smile, "we are a cultural mission, not the C.I.A. or M.I.5. Secondly, a low-key approach suits the circumstances, since we are at this stage just following up a rumor. Moreover, young students are everywhere and unlikely to arouse suspicion. The cost to us is also minimal, as our recruits are to be paid expenses only, plus a bonus on results."

"What you say seems quite reasonable," his colleague judiciously agreed. "But how do these amateurs know where to begin their quest?"

Matsuo Yamoto returned a conspiratorial smile, saying:

"The London correspondent of one of our national dailies, Hideo Nagano, informed me that several British Sunday newspapers have, very much on the quiet, assigned investigative journalists to follow up the rumor. It seems that a bronze animal head was included in the published will of a Scottish army officer who was a direct descendent of a certain Iain Hamilton, a colonel in a Scottish guards regiment who took part in the Opium Wars during the latter part of the nineteenth century."

"Wasn't the sculpture's value realized after probate, along with the deceased officer's other assets?" Issiguru asked.

"The problem, Akira, is that the executor of Hamilton's estate, Lothian Bank, has filed for bankruptcy in a Scottish court. Until that process is completed – and it may take weeks, if not months – the bank's records are frozen. It seems, however, that some of the assets – paintings, books, for example, as opposed to financial investments - were realized just ahead of the bankruptcy filing."

"So the investigative journalists are now scouring Scotland to determine where the bronze might now reside?"

"Quite so, Akira. The assumption seems to be that an art gallery, or similar institution, may have acquired it, possibly for re-sale. Hideo Nagano, from the grapevine in British journalism, seems fairly sure that would be its likeliest destination."

"So your team of boy scouts is shadowing the journalists?" a partly intrigued, partly amused Akira Issiguru asked.

Matsuo Yamoto judiciously nodded.

"They are all currently in Scotland. We are assuming that one of the journalists, given their track record in exposing all manner of devious activities, will eventually locate the bronze. That is where you come in, honored friend."

"You mean, Matsuo, that once the bronze's whereabouts are discovered, I am to obtain it, by force if necessary?"

"And bring it here to Canary Wharf for safe storage, until the opportune time for us to return it to its rightful owners, the Chinese."

"Would it not be better to use it as a bargaining chip in our dispute over the Siriaku Islands?"

The mission head looked a little bemused at that remark and said:

"That is something for our foreign service to determine, Akira. My instructions thus far are to keep it in a secure location."

"You could drop a strong hint in the right quarters, Matsuo," his visitor said. "Meanwhile, I am to kick my heels here in London until you hear back from one of your amateur sleuths?"

"London is a fascinating city, Akira," the other replied, "with limitless resources for your entertainment. And some excellent restaurants. What did Dr. Johnson say?"

"A man who is tired of London is tired of life," came the pat retort.

*

Lingering over breakfast in the dining-room of Cairngorm Hotel, George Mason scanned the pages of *The Scotsman*, while his companion tackled a crossword puzzle. It was raining steadily outside as the commuter traffic built along Sauchiehall Street, one of Glasgow's main arteries. Checking his watch, the detective laid aside his newspaper and crossed to the foyer, figuring that by now – it was just turned nine o'clock – both Cecil Weeks and Chief Inspector Harrington would be at their respective desks. He decided to ring the magazine editor first, mainly to find out if his separated wife Vera had used their joint credit card since her purchase of a landscape painting at Arklet Studio in Inversnaid. Immediately afterwards, he called his chief.

"Any developments, Inspector?" the senior officer testily enquired.

"Irina Carmichael and I have ascertained that Vera Weeks recently visited Tobermory and Inversnaid," Mason informed him.

"Isle of Mull and Loch Lomond, if I am not mistaken," the other remarked. "Quite an interesting jaunt you are having up there in the Highlands, Inspector. Productive, I hope?"

"We discovered that Vera Weeks interviewed a suspected art forger on Mull, whom we have ruled out of our immediate enquiries. She also made a rather expensive purchase at an art studio in Inversnaid."

"What exactly are you referring to, Inspector?"

"A Chinese bronze sculpture, in the form of a dog's head."

Bill Harrington grunted.

"Is that meant to be mean something?" he enquired.

"It may well be, Chief Inspector," Mason replied. "Prior to completing the purchase, the Weeks woman needed to make certain financial arrangements, possibly with her bank. If we knew who made the transfer to her account, it might give further clues to her agenda."

"How did you happen to light on Inversnaid?" his intrigued senior asked.

"We were able to access her Visa transactions, via her husband Cecil, with whom she has maintained a joint account."

"Keep following the credit then, Inspector. You will catch up with her sooner or later. The sooner the better, in fact, since there is pressing business back here at the Yard."

"There may be a problem with that," Mason replied. "I just now rang Cecil Weeks at his office in London. He edits the music magazine, *Nocturne*."

"I have often read it," the other said. "My wife subscribes to it. They just did a broad preview of this season's Promenade Concerts at the Albert Hall."

"Cecil told me that there are no new Visa expenses recorded since Inversnaid, where Vera bought a landscape painting. Irina told me that her sister generally preferred to use cash or check."

"So the trail has gone cold?" Harrington grumbled.

"It would appear so, for the time being at least."

"Where are you now, exactly?"

"At Cairngorm Hotel, Glasgow."

"Then you had both better return to London, to await developments. No use kicking your heels north of the border. There is a new case you can look into, meanwhile. Detective Sergeant Aubrey has already made a useful start."

George Mason rather glumly put the phone down and returned to his table. He hated to leave a case unsolved, but such were the pressures of police business that he had no doubt his plate would be full again on his return to base. The thought of teaming up again with Alison Aubrey momentarily cheered him.

"I do not mind at all," Irina remarked, on hearing the news. "I do really need to get back to Geoffrey and also contact my publisher. We shall take things from there. Something is almost sure to appear on her credit card sooner or later."

"I shall go check the train times at Reception," he said, draining his coffee. "You should be back in Christchurch in time for dinner."

"I should like to invite you at some point, Inspector," Irina said, "to meet my husband and see something of our beautiful city."

"I would love to do that," the pleasantly surprised detective replied. "Perhaps after all this business is settled, I could bring my wife Adele down for the day."

"You would be very welcome," she assured him.

*

Towards noon, Keino Sato eased his hire car onto the parking lot of Scafell Pike Inn, switched off the motor and sat quietly for a few moments before alighting and negotiating the main street of Keswick, a busy market town some distance south of the Scottish border. The aroma of freshly-baked scones and pastries drew him to a small café furnished country-style, where he ordered coffee to refresh himself after his long drive. The early-morning rain had cleared and the sidewalks were filling with tourists drawn to the area during the summer months. Many of them, he noticed, wore hiking gear suitable for exploring the fells and dales of the Lake District. He noticed Japanese nationals too. Since they were not dressed for outdoor pursuits, he assumed they were here on the organized tours popular with his countrymen. Their main objective was Dove Cottage, William Wordsworth's home at Grasmere, as well as his grave in the local churchyard. The celebrated Romantic poet, born in 1770, was very highly rated in Japan. Keino was well-acquainted with his work, from his high school studies in English Literature.

As he sipped his French roast, he reflected on the circumstances that had brought him here. A second-year student of sociology at Lancaster University, not very far south of the English lakes, he had noted with much interest an item on the student notice-board. It read: *Attractive summer employment opportunity for undergraduates of Asian origin.* Included, was a London telephone number. He had discussed it with his English girlfriend Janice, a first-year student of French and German at Lancaster University, who encouraged him to apply, as she herself was heading to the south of France for the grape harvest. She would be joining him this afternoon to go boating on nearby Derwentwater. They planned to have dinner together afterwards before parting for the summer.

On answering the advertisement, he found himself two days later at Canary Wharf, London. An official at the Japanese Cultural Mission, Matsuo Yamoto, had offered him the position after an interview the young man felt had mainly focused on his sense of patriotism and financial probity. The assignment was to remain highly confidential, in that it served important national interests. Keino had readily accepted. It seemed to him like the sort of undercover work one normally read about only in spy novels. A rail pass of one month's duration was issued to him, plus three hundred pounds to cover expenses, including car rentals when necessary. His task was carefully explained to him: he was to shadow the movements of a noted investigative journalist named Vera Weeks and report back to Yamoto. It was not necessary for him to understand the motives behind this assignment, which he was not to discuss with his family or even with his closest friends.

Janice would try her level best to get some inkling into what she rightly considered a most unusual, even exciting, vacation employment. Keino would remain mum, with a self-satisfied air, conscious that he was temporarily much better off financially than he had been in the last two years on a student stipend. He finished his coffee and headed back to Scafell Pike Inn, where he reserved a room for the night. Since he could not occupy it before late-afternoon, he used the telephone booth in the lobby to place a call to London.

"Good to hear from you again, Keino," Matsuo Yamoto said. "How are things going?"

"I have some news to report," the student excitedly replied. "The journalist Vera Weeks has just booked into Scafell Pike Inn at Keswick after driving down from Glasgow. Before that, she visited Inversnaid, on Loch Lomond."

"What transpired at Inversnaid, Keino?"

"She had a wooden crate loaded into the back of her car. Something she had bought at an art studio there."

There was a brief pause, while the information sank in.

"Are you sure of these facts, my young friend?"

"Absolutely. I managed to park my car directly behind hers and saw her enter Arklet Studio. After a while, she re-emerged and visited a local café. Following a quick lunch, she returned to the studio and made what I assume was a purchase from stock."

"Do you have any idea of the contents of the crate?"

"Afraid not, Mr. Yamoto, except to say that is was a quite large object."

The mission head turned to Akira Issiguru with a broad smile, saying:

"It seems like one of our boy scouts, as you derisively termed them, has turned up trumps. He was detailed to track Vera Weeks, a prominent investigative journalist employed by *The Sunday Post*. She has booked a room at Scafell Pike Inn at a place called Keswick."

"The English Lakes?" an intrigued Akira remarked. "It is my very favorite part of this country. I know it well."

"You are to go up there without delay, Akira, and take over from young Sato. Weeks is apparently carrying a crated object bought at an art studio in Inversnaid."

"Nothing would give me more pleasure," the other replied, "than a trip to Keswick. It will bring back many memories."

Returning to the telephone, Yamoto advised his young scout to keep a low profile and await the arrival of an agent from London, assuring him of a substantial cash bonus if his information was found to be of value to them.

Feeling well-pleased with himself, Keino Sato quit the inn and set off on foot to the railway station, checking on the way that his quarry's car was still on the inn parking lot. Within the hour, he met Janice off the Lancaster train. They took a quick snack at the station buffet before heading off for an afternoon's rowing on Derwentwater, to his mind one of the most beautiful of the English lakes, with the high peaks of the Cumbrian Mountains in the background. The sky had mainly cleared, allowing the afternoon sun to appear through drifting banks of cumulus.

"So how is your summer job proceeding?" Janice asked him, as they paused in the center of the broad lake to rest their arms a while.

"Too early to say," her boyfriend evasively replied. He was not about to tell her that he had traced his quarry from Edinburgh to the Isle of Mull, and from there to the Scottish Highlands, before following her down to Keswick.

"What exactly does your job involve, Keino?' Janice probed, as they spotted a fork-tailed kite swooping low over the water.

"It is a type of research project, Janice," was all he would say.

On leaving the lake late-afternoon, they explored the shops along the main street of Keswick. Janice took the opportunity to purchase a few toiletries, while her boyfriend was mainly interested in craft shops and art stores selling paintings of Lakeland scenes. As the clock moved towards seven, their thoughts turned to dinner. Keino wanted it to be something of an occasion, it being their last evening together for several weeks. He had some reservations, however, when Janice pressed him to eat at his hotel, since he fully imagined that Vera Weeks would use the same restaurant this evening. It might be risky to come out into the open, after spending days in the shadows. In the end, his desire to please his girlfriend and his confidence in the low profile he had been able to maintain at a number of places in Scotland, persuaded him to accede to her wishes. It would be a four-course dinner with wine at Scafell Pike Inn, followed by coffee and liqueurs, or his name was not Keino Sato.

Twenty minutes ahead of him, Vera Weeks took the lift down to the dining-room, having applied minimal make-up in her third-floor room and donned a plain cotton dress. She was pleased to note that the restaurant was only half-full, and that the windows were part-open to admit an evening breeze resembling a minor zephyr on this warm June day. She chose a table in the far corner of the room and scanned the menu, opting for tomato bisque, followed by roast pheasant with jacket potato and endive salad. To accompany it, she chose a half-bottle of Chardonnay, which was served almost immediately, and listened appreciatively as the resident pianist launched into a program of Chopin mazurkas.

She sipped the chilled wine appreciatively – it was of New Zealand vintage - while perusing the latest edition of *Nocturne*, which she had managed to obtain the previous day at a newspaper kiosk in Glasgow. She was eager to read her husband's preview of the London concert season, especially the Promenade Concerts scheduled at the Royal Albert Hall. Dear old Cecil, she mused. How did he manage without her, she wondered, aware that it was her own need for mental space that had moved them apart on a trial separation? That he was still in love with her, she had few doubts. That he would console himself in the arms of the young member of his editorial staff who was infatuated with him, she also doubted. Cecil's hallmark was loyalty and the British stiff upper-lip, the latter being a quality that she, as the granddaughter of White Russian émigrés eventually moving to England from France, had some difficulty appreciating.

Having done full justice to the entrée, she pondered the dessert offerings. On glancing up to catch the eye of the waiter, an elderly man with a slight limp, she spotted a young Asian man, accompanied by what she took to be an English companion, about to occupy a table on the far side of the room. His appearance on the scene arrested her attention. He looked vaguely familiar. Had she seen him before, she wondered? As the waiter hovered in her vicinity, it suddenly struck her that he had been in Tobermory on the day she had interviewed the local artist, Rory MacTaggart. She had also noticed him at Inversnaid, sitting behind the wheel of a small Ford sedan parked directly behind her rental car outside Arklet Studio. She did not recall seeing him in Glasgow, where she had spent two days visiting art galleries. To spot him here, for the third time in a matter of days, struck her as an extraordinary coincidence. Perhaps it was more than coincidence, she mused.

Not inclined to take any chances, she rose slowly from her place while the young couple were engaged in weighing up the menu. She then left the restaurant by a side-door, went up to her room and quickly packed her valise. Fifteen minutes later, she took the lift down to the foyer, settled her bill and booked accommodation at a sister hotel farther down the coast. Retrieving her car from the parking lot, she left Keswick and sped into the night.

*

Akira Issiguru rose early the following morning, took breakfast in his hotel room and availed himself of the sauna amenity in the basement, before embarking on a small shopping expedition in the West End, mainly to wire anniversary flowers to his wife via Interflora. It was past noon when he arrived at Euston Station to catch the mainline express to Carlisle, where he was met mid-evening by Keino Sato. The young student was a little awed by this new arrival on the scene and would have liked to quiz him about the motives behind these 007-style activities. The contents of the wooden crate and its importance to national interests also exercised his mind, and he would have liked to pose questions. Something in the other man's demeanor, however, restrained him. He spent most of the hour-long drive back to Keswick, in thinning tourist traffic, answering queries about his college studies, career options and the like. The older man, for his part, expatiated with evident pleasure on his own time as a post-graduate student in London, assuring Keino that a British degree would stand him in good stead back home and give him an edge in a difficult employment market.

As Issiguru had not eaten since breakfast, they called at a pub in Grasmere for an early dinner, lingering over pints of Theakston's Ale after their game pie and French fries, so as to reach Keswick after nightfall. On eventually entering the parking lot of Scafell Pike Inn, which was bordered by birch trees, the agent asked Keino to point out Vera Weeks's car. The bewildered student glanced around in disbelief. The spaces were nearly all occupied, but there was no sign the woman's sedan.

Issiguru gave Keino a wry glance.

"Seems like the bird has flown," he said, irritably re-pocketing the alarm disabler he had intended to use while entering the journalist's vehicle.

"She *was* here," Keino insisted. "I noticed her at dinner in the restaurant last evening."

"Let us check with Reception," the other said, striding quickly towards the main entrance, bidding his companion to remain outside.

"I have a dinner appointment with one of your guests," he informed the duty clerk. "Could you inform her of my arrival?"

"Her name?" the woman asked, consulting the register.

"Vera Weeks."

"Mrs. Weeks left at short notice yesterday evening," the clerk explained.

The Japanese frowned in disappointment.

"I expect something urgent cropped up," he said, with affected regret. "Our dinner date was made some time ago."

The clerk returned a sympathetic look, taken in by his mock-sincerity.

"Do you happen to know where she was headed?" he politely asked.

The clerk's eyes narrowed.

"I am not at liberty to discuss our guests' private affairs," she tartly replied.

Akira Issiguru reached inside his jacket pocket and pulled out a twenty-pound banknote, sliding it across the counter. The clerk eyed it cagily and glanced uncertainly at the visitor. He struck her as respectable enough, clad in a dark business suit and club tie.

"This is very irregular," she said in a low voice, while pocketing the banknote. "Vera Weeks booked ahead to our sister hotel, The Dunes, at Lytham St. Anne's."

"Thank you very much for your assistance," Akira Issiguru said, promptly taking his leave.

CHAPTER 5

Olivier Breton rose early on the morning of June 16. He prepared a simple breakfast of coffee and croissants in his bachelor apartment at Pantin, a banlieue of north-eastern Paris. It was hardly the most fashionable quarter of the city, being home to a mixed population that included North Africans, Asians and East Europeans. The ethnic mix strongly appealed to him, having served overseas with the French army in several former French colonies. The restaurants and food stores had a fascinating variety of offerings, and there had been few incidents of racial conflict. Immigrants from many different countries mingled harmoniously enough, without abandoning their respective customs, style of dress and traditions.   After showering, he donned a dark suit and matching tie, fed his parrot Asterix and quit the apartment to cover on foot the short distance to the Metro station. Pantin, he was pleased to note as he stepped up his gait, was becoming increasingly gentrified.

Improvements to the canal leading north from the Seine had created swaths of welcome greenery, with appealing canal-side cafes. The old mills and warehouses of the industrial era had been converted into modern office suites for companies like Chanel, or into ateliers for artists and fashion designers. He felt that his colleagues, who generally lived in the more up-market suburbs or in dormitory towns along the Seine, envied him for the variety and affordability of his locale. But they would never admit it and their wives often shuddered at mere mention of the name. Pantin, to his mind, was on the up-and-up.

Greeting the purveyor of organic foods, who was setting up his store-front display on Rue Eloise, he entered the Metro station, bought a copy of *Le Monde* to read on the journey into the heart of the city and eventually alighted at St. Germain-des-Pres. From there, he strode to the offices of the Directorate on Rue Theophile Gauthier. The director, Louis Dutourd, a long-time stalwart of the security services, was waiting for him.

"*Bonjour, Olivier,*" he said, in greeting.

"*Bonjour, Monsieur Dutourd,*" the other returned.

"I have something that may interest you," the director began, "in view of your previous experience in the Far East."

"And what might that be?" Olivier Breton enquired, immediately interested.

"Our contact at the Japanese Cultural Mission in London has informed me that a special agent from Japan has recently arrived in England. She managed to eavesdrop on his conference with Matsuo Yamoto, the mission head."

"The agent's name?" Breton asked.

"Akira Issiguru."

"I think I may have come across him before. He was in Seoul, I believe, not too long ago, in connection with compensation for war-time Korean comfort women. Unless I am confusing him with someone else."

"His brief in Britain is of a rather different character," Dutourd pointedly remarked. "You will recall, Olivier, that we returned to the Chinese two bronze sculptures that were looted by Western troops from the Zodiac Fountain in the courtyard of the Imperial Summer Palace at Beijing?"

"I do indeed," the other replied. "An effigy of a rat and of a rabbit, if I remember rightly, that disappeared during the Opium Wars."

The director nodded.

"There is a rumor," he continued, "that a third bronze may have come to light. Nothing definitive, so far, according to our sources, but we cannot afford to overlook it."

"What would Japan's interest be in that?" a puzzled Olivier Breton queried.

Louis Dutourd shrugged his broad shoulders.

"Anybody's guess," he replied. "Unless it has something to do with their current dispute with China over the Siriaku Islands."

"As a bargaining chip?"

"Possibly."

Breton sat back in his chair and pondered the situation. This was something tailor-made for his background and interests. The look in his eye confirmed the director's view that he was engaging the right person for the job.

"Do I detect a degree of interest in this assignment?" he wryly enquired.

"What precisely is the assignment?" Olivier Breton asked.

"Your brief is to shadow Issiguru and see where the trail leads. Our Ministry of Culture is very anxious that, if such an artifact has in fact resurfaced, it must reside at the Louvre, temporarily at least. Until such time as we see fit to return it to the Chinese."

"On the grounds that it will greatly benefit our mutual relationship, as well as improving our trading prospects?"

"*Sans doute, mon ami.*"

"That can only be a good thing, Monsieur le Directeur, to help us get out of this long-drawn-out recession."

"The green shoots are just now beginning to appear," Louis Dutourd said. "The Minister of Trade is counting on us to bring off a coup in this matter, since the Far East has become a rapidly developing market for European goods."

"So when do I start?" the eager agent asked.

"As soon as convenient. Tomorrow, if possible. Take the Eurostar to London and ring me as soon as you arrive. Our contact has given us the name of Issiguru's cellphone company. They have agreed to inform us of the dates and locations of his calls, enabling you to keep track of his movements."

"The benefits of modern technology," Breton said.

"All intelligence services avail themselves of it," Dutourd said. "And, by the way, the name of our contact at Canary Wharf is Yuki Kimura. Arrange a meeting with her as soon as convenient."

*

That same morning, George Mason left his West London home by car with his wife Adele. Normally, he would have taken the Underground to Westminster, but on this occasion Adele had shopping to do in the West End. He relaxed as she took the wheel to join the stream of commuter traffic, just now beginning to tail off as it was already turned nine o'clock.

"Drop me off at Bond Street," he said. "You will then be able to use the multi-story parking facility behind Selfridge's."

"What time shall I expect you home for dinner?" she asked.

"Usual time...around six."

"Sure you won't be summoned to the Hebrides, in the meantime, or some other remote location?" Adele ironically quipped.

Her husband laughed at that remark, fully aware of what she had to put up with married to a member of the C.I.D. His job often played havoc with domestic routines, with its unpredictable hours and short-notice assignments, certainly round Britain and Europe, if not the globe. But she adapted well, he considered, pursuing her own interests and cultivating a close circle of friends, for bridge evenings, keep-fit activities and the like.

"I haven't been in touch with Irina Carmichael since the Scottish trip," he said. "Did I mention that she writes historical novels?"

"You did not, George," Adele replied. "Sounds very interesting."

"Her current area of interest, she informed me, is the Tudor era."

"Always fertile ground," came the reply.

"Specifically, she is into the reign of Mary 1, who married Philip of Spain."

"Presumably because her mother, Catharine of Aragon, was also Spanish."

"Some of her closest advisers," her husband said, "urged her to marry the Earl of Devon, Edward Courtenay, a descendant of the Plantagenet kings. They feared that England would become a mere lackey of Spain if she chose Philip."

"Didn't the Plantagenets immediately precede the Tudors?"

The detective nodded.

"The last of the line was Richard 111," he said. "He was slain in battle with Henry Tudor at Bosworth Field. They recently found his remains under a parking lot at Leicester that had formerly been part of a monastery complex."

"I do believe they have resolved the dispute over where to re-bury his remains," Adele said. "Leicester Cathedral has been chosen, denying the claims of York Minster."

"Fascinating, what turns up just by excavating building sites. Layers of history, dating back to pre-Roman times."

"Since Richard was a Yorkist," Adele remarked, "many parties in Yorkshire will be disappointed that Leicester prevailed."

"True enough," her husband said, on alighting from the car at Bond Street. "I shall see you back home at six. Enjoy your day."

With that, he strode to the nearest Underground station and took the tube to Charing Cross. From there, it was a short walk along The Strand to Fleet Street and the editorial office of *The Sunday Post,* which he reached shortly after ten o'clock. Auberon Maclintock was expecting him.

"Good morning, Inspector Mason," the editor said, rising from his chair.

"Good day, Mr. Maclintock."

"Please take a seat," the other said. "To what do I owe the honor of your visit today?" There was just a hint of irony in his voice.

"I am here regarding your key journalist, Vera Weeks."

"Vera, of course!" Maclintock exclaimed. "I thought it might be that."

"Her sister Irina and I traced her recent movements from Edinburgh to Tobermory on the Island of Mull, and subsequently to Inversnaid," the detective said. "It seems she spent a large sum of money on a bronze sculpture representing a dog's head."

The editor rose to his feet, in evident excitement.

"You are saying she has actually located the bronze, Inspector?" he asked.

His visitor returned a look of surprise at the man's upbeat reaction and waited for an explanation. The editor left his desk and paced up and down the room, quite beside himself.

"You have the advantage of me," a bemused George Mason remarked.

Maclintock regained his seat and glanced in triumph at his Scotland Yard visitor.

"I feel I owe you some explanation," he said.

"I believe you do," Mason curtly replied.

"A short while ago," the editor said, "a rumor arose that a long-lost bronze sculpture from the Zodiac Fountain in Beijing had resurfaced. Every Sunday newspaper in this country has, on the quiet, sent an investigative reporter to look into the matter, in an attempt to establish the facts. And now you are telling me, Inspector Mason, that our own Vera Weeks has done just that! I am well and truly flabbergasted, but I am not really all that surprised."

His visitor returned a quizzical smile.

"But you did not inform her husband Cecil or her sister Irina of any of this," he complained.

"Vera and I simply did not want anyone to know," came the reply. "It was a very hush-hush assignment. We wanted to gain the edge on our competitors."

"A scoop, in other words?"

"Precisely, Inspector," the editor said. "You understand the pressures on the newspaper industry these days, with increasing competition from the internet and other media."

"I understand perfectly," George Mason replied.

"Besides," Maclintock went on, "I had no idea the police would be involved. My apologies if I caused you any inconvenience."

"Not a problem," the detective magnanimously allowed. "The main consideration now is Vera Weeks's current whereabouts and safety."

"You have lost the scent?"

"We managed to track her initially by credit card transactions that Cecil Weeks can access by a quick telephone-call. But she has not used her Visa in the past few days."

"How about her cellphone?" Maclintock asked. "Surely you can access that with all the modern technology at your disposal?"

"She has not apparently used that either," the detective replied.

Auberon Maclintock pondered the situation for a few moments, his euphoria over discovery of the bronze slowly evaporating.

"We need to locate her soon," he emphasized. "We cannot publish anything in the *Post* until we have seen the sculpture and had its authenticity independently verified."

"No scoop yet, then?" Mason drily observed.

"Not for this week's edition, at any rate. The problem, Inspector, is that there are so many fakes on the art market, particularly originating in China."

"I understand that to be the case, Mr. Maclintock, although that is not my concern. We have a specialist art fraud unit at the Yard."

"We could not publish anything until we are absolutely certain of the bronze's provenance," the editor went on, laboring the point. "An expert from the British Museum, for example, would fit the bill."

"Something else that puzzles me, Mr. Maclintock, is the financial aspect. Where would someone of Vera's means find the resources for such a purchase?"

The editor shrugged his shoulders, looking completely stumped.

"It certainly did not come from this office," he remarked. "We barely turn a profit as it is. Equally puzzling to me, however, is her failure to communicate her discovery to me. After all, we are the ones who initiated this project."

"A valid point," George Mason agreed, rising to take his leave. "Perhaps she is much better-off thank you think."

The editor returned a skeptical look at that remark.

"Perhaps. Perhaps not," he said. "But you *will* keep me posted, won't you, Inspector, about any developments?"

"I shall certainly do my best," the detective assured him. "Although this case is taking on the character of a Chinese puzzle."

"You can say that again!" the editor agreed.

*

On leaving Scafell Pike Inn, Akira Issiguru considered it too late to proceed to Lytham St. Anne's, a genteel resort town on England's northwest coast, not very far south of more boisterous Blackpool, the so-called 'playground of the north'. At Keino Sato's suggestion, they drove down to Lancaster, where they both spent the night of June 15 at the student's university apartment. The next morning, Keino took him to the student cafeteria for breakfast. This greatly appealed to the special agent, not so much for the menu, which was typical institutional catering, but for the experience of reliving his own halcyon days, two decades ago, as a post-graduate student in London. The restaurant was more sparsely occupied than in term time, remaining open with a skeleton staff for people on residential summer courses. The morning sun shone fitfully through the gauze curtains, auguring a brighter day ahead.

After the meal, Issiguru warmly thanked his host. He had no further use for him now that he had identified the target. In fact, he would more likely be a hindrance. It was time for the amateur to give way to the professional.

"Now we must part company, my young friend," he said, lighting a filter cigarette as they strolled towards the parking lot.

Keino Sato returned a look of surprise, tinged with pique. If he had thought that his cloak-and-dagger adventure of the last few days was going to continue indefinitely, he had obviously been mistaken. He had begun to relish the role, the like of which he had seen played out countless times on the cinema screen. There would be no use protesting; his compatriot would be unmoved. His only regret was that he did not know – probably would never know - the contents of the crate that the Englishwoman had placed in her car trunk at Inversnaid.

"You have done very well, my young friend," Issiguru generously conceded. "All you need do now is return this vehicle to the rental company where you hired it, so that I can get a new one. If our little enterprise is successful, Mr. Yamoto will send you a generous bonus for the constructive part you have played."

That encouraging remark was music to the younger man's ears, giving him visions of a vacation with his girlfriend Janice on the French Riviera. He could meet up with her after her grape-picking venture and book accommodation at some high-end resort like St. Tropez or Antibes.

"In fact," the older man continued, as the rental car nosed onto the highway, "you might wish to consider a career in the secret service when you have finished your studies. A knowledge of foreign languages and cultures, such as you will have gained in England, would be invaluable."

That was more music to Keino Sato's ears; in fact, it was a choral symphony. And in today's employment environment, the prospect of immediately finding a position with the Japanese government was very appealing.

"I should like that very much, sir," he replied.

"Contact the foreign ministry, in due course," the other said, "and mention my name."

"I will certainly give that some serious thought," Keino assured him, not quite sure how Janice would take to the idea of settling in Japan, in the event that they got married.

As they neared the car rental, Issiguru turned to him and said:

"Do you think the Englishwoman may have noticed you at Scafell Pike Inn?"

"I think not, sir," the student replied.

"You do not sound so sure, Keino. Did you, for example, also enter the dining-room for dinner?"

The student nodded uneasily.

"That may have been unwise, Keino," the older man said. "Something must have prompted her to leave the inn at such short notice, given that she had booked in for the night. She may have smelled a rat."

"Perhaps she was called away urgently," Keino countered. "A family emergency, for instance."

"I do hope you are right, my young friend."

Keino Sato then fished in his jacket pocket for the registration number of the journalist's car and handed it to the older man, who bade him adieu and entered the rental office. Twenty minutes later, all paperwork completed, Issiguru drove a brand-new Volvo in a south-westerly direction towards the coast, through the undulating contours of the English countryside. On reaching Blackpool, a noted resort he had not previously visited, he parked his car near a structure somewhat resembling the Eifel Tower, crossed over the busy tramway and stretched his legs on the promenade fronting the Golden Mile of sandy beach. Near the height of the summer season, it was full of vacationers and day-trippers, mainly family groups with small children building sandcastles, playing ball games or indulging in that curious European habit of sunbathing. A few hardier souls ventured into the incoming tide of the Irish Sea. As he walked, taking in the sea air and the holiday atmosphere, he mused on the best way to achieve his objective. If Vera Weeks's car was locked – the likeliest scenario – forcing the trunk would activate the alarm. He would need to disable it quickly, probably during dinner service when the parking lot would likely be deserted. He would have preferred the cover of darkness, but in mid-June dusk would not descend until after ten o'clock. The alternative would be to wait until nightfall before recovering the bronze, a less appealing option involving a long wait. He would see how the land lay, he decided, on reaching the Dunes Hotel. Opting to spend the afternoon in Blackpool, before completing the short drive south to Lytham St. Anne's, he directed his steps towards North Pier, contemplating an *al fresco* lunch of fish-and-chips.

He arrived at Dunes Hotel shortly after seven o'clock, circling the parking lot to identify the vehicle driven by Vera Weeks. By a stroke of luck, it was parked beneath a large overhanging beech tree on the far side of the lot, some distance from the hotel. There was a vacant spot next to it. Reversing his Volvo into it and glancing round to make sure the area was deserted, he jimmied the trunk and peered inside, fully expecting to discover a large wooden crate. As the car alarm beeped insistently, he quickly disabled it before scrambling back into his own vehicle and speeding back towards the center of Lytham, conscious of a car trunk holding only hiking boots, an umbrella and a watercolor painting of a Scottish Highland scene.

Relieved that no one had spotted him, he eventually parked his Volvo near the archaic windmill that dominated the grassy sea-front, stepped out and lit a panatela. A few people strolled the area with their dogs. They paid him no attention, as he sat on a bench looking out to sea to collect his thoughts, suppressing feelings of anger against Keino Sato. Yamoto was to blame, he decided, for hiring rank amateurs. After a while, he took out his cellphone and rang the apartment the mission head occupied at Mayfair.

"Good evening, honored friend," Yamoto said, on recognizing the special agent's voice. "How are things progressing?"

"Our young friend Sato has misled us, I am afraid," Issiguru replied. "Vera Weeks is by no means carrying a wooden crate in the trunk of her car."

"But Keino assured me that it was placed there at Inversnaid. He saw it with his own eyes."

"If that is truly the case, which I doubt," the irritated special agent said, "she has since disposed of it."

There was a pause, as Matsuo Yamoto considered the implications of this unexpected development.

"That is certainly a possibility," he at length agreed. "And, if that is indeed the case, you will need to shadow her closely. It could be that she arranged for it to be shipped on, and that Sato failed to take note of the fact."

"Which comes from employing amateurs, honorable colleague," Issiguru sourly remarked.

"Let me remind you, Akira," the other countered, "that the existence of the bronze was pure speculation up to a few days ago. Keino Sato has at least confirmed its resurfacing and identified a purchaser. It is up to you to ascertain its present whereabouts. So where are you now, exactly?"

"At Lytham St. Anne's, a quiet resort on the northwest coast, just south of Blackpool."

"And where is Mrs. Weeks?"

"She is staying at the Dunes Hotel, on the outskirts of the town."

"When she departs, Akira," Matsuo Yamoto said, "make sure you keep her in your sights. As for young Sato, we shall dispense with his services."

"I already did so," came the tart reply. "He has returned to his student digs at Lancaster."

CHAPTER 6

Vera Weeks slept until nine o'clock, following her late arrival from Keswick the previous evening. After showering, she dressed quickly and went down to the dining-room of Dunes Hotel to catch the end of the breakfast sitting. It was a buffet service of cold and warm dishes, most of the latter having already been consumed by earlier risers. She settled for grapefruit, lukewarm poached eggs and coffee. As she ate, she scanned the headlines of *The Guardian*, paying scant attention to the handful of other late risers scattered around the room, including an Asian of short stature engrossed in a copy of *The Daily Telegraph*, which obscured his features.

Noting that fresh coffee had just arrived, she crossed to the service area to replenish her cup, choosing a Danish pastry to accompany it. On eventually rising from table, she went out to her car to retrieve her umbrella. The sky had darkened, threatening rain, and she had in mind a visit to the Lytham bookstores, to see if they had any new publications on aspects of the art world that particularly interested her.

On reaching her vehicle, she noted with horror that the trunk had been forced. Making a quick check of her belongings, she realized with relief that nothing appeared to be missing. That struck her as very odd, as she retraced her steps to the hotel, went up to her room and pondered the matter. Could it be simple opportunism, she wondered? That was not uncommon in parking lots, and more prevalent nowadays on account of the economic recession. Or was the thief looking for something specific, that he or she did not find?

Her thoughts turned again to the young Asian she had first noticed hanging around the harbor at Tobermory, then again at Inversnaid. Incredible, it seemed to her, that he should have turned up yet again in the dining-room of Scafell Pike Inn. Could that same individual have followed her here? And, if so, how on earth could he have divined her itinerary? No, that scenario was too far-fetched even to consider. Crossing to the window overlooking the gray expanse of ocean and peering at the threatening sky, she decided that the break-in was most likely a random act. Before venturing out into the uncertain weather, she placed a call on the room telephone to the Russian Consulate at Cardiff.

"May I speak with Ilya Sorotkin?" she enquired, as the line became live.

"Be kind to wait one moment," came the reply, in unidiomatic English.

Vera's short wait was soon rewarded by the familiar voice of the consular official requesting the name of his caller.

"Vera Weeks," she announced.

"Good morning, Vera," Sorotkin said. "How are things with you, since we last spoke?"

"I managed to secure the item you are interested in," she replied, "following on the financial arrangements you were able to provide."

"Amazing, Vera," the official replied, "that you were able to light on the bronze so quickly and steal a march on the other journalists trying to locate it. My congratulations."

"A lucky break, Ilya," she modestly replied. "I figured that a sculpture owned by a Scottish family and disposed of by Scottish executors, namely Lothian Bank, would wind up in a gallery not too far from where its owner resided. I visited several places in central Scotland, in fact, before going to Inversnaid. I have had previous dealings with Arklet Studio, who seem to have a knack of finding rare and unusual objects. They also deal occasionally in Oriental art. The proprietor, of course, had no idea of the provenance of the bronze, or of its true value. It must be worth at least twice the sum I paid."

"You did well, Vera, and we are most grateful. Our relationship with China has been improving in recent years, after a series of border disputes. We are notably increasing trade with them, exchanging official visits and engaging in joint military exercises. It augurs well for the future. If we can now return one of the missing Zodiac bronzes, that can only boost these positive trends."

"We can steal a march on the French, too," Vera added. "They will be falling over themselves to add a third bronze, following their return of the rat and the rabbit."

"That must be prevented at all costs," Sorotkin remarked. "Where is the dog effigy now?"

"In the safe hands of National Freight Services, on its way to Cardiff's Elizabeth Dock," she informed him. "I consigned it in Glasgow two days ago. They told me it would take several days, since the transport takes a circuitous route to reach Wales, making overnight stops on the way."

"Reasonable enough, Vera," the consular official said. "You preferred that method to driving down with it yourself?"

"To be honest, Ilya, I did, even though I might have saved time. I considered it risky carrying such a valuable item in my car. As a matter of fact, my car trunk was forced open only yesterday evening."

"You don't say so!" the other exclaimed.

"I think it was a random, opportunist event," the journalist said. "Unless, of course, I was specifically targeted."

"By whom, for instance?"

"Are you aware, Ilya, of a possible Japanese interest in the bronze?"

"Absolutely not, Vera. I doubt they even know it has resurfaced. Few people do. But even if they are aware of the fact, I do not see how they would wish to obtain it. What possible use would it be to Japan, embroiled as they are in disputes over a group of barren islands in the South China Sea?"

Vera Weeks chuckled to herself at that remark, dismissing in her mind any connection between the ubiquitous young Asian and the Zodiac bronze. His frequent appearances must have been just remarkable coincidences, she decided.

"When is the freighter *Svoboda* due to dock at Cardiff?" she asked.

"Svezda Lines runs a weekly service between Cardiff and St. Petersburg. It is slated to arrive here on June 20. I double-checked its schedule with the port authority. Your crate will be placed on board, under guard, the moment it reaches the dock. A private berth has been reserved for you in the crew's quarters."

"Perfect," Vera Weeks said.

"When you arrive at St. Petersburg, there will be television interviews followed by an official reception. The short series of lectures you have been invited to give will commence June 26."

"I have carefully prepared my material," the journalist assured him. "What about the accommodation arrangements?"

"A small suite of rooms has been reserved for you at the Marski, one of our leading hotels. Many foreign visitors, such as businessmen, authors and musicians, stay there. You will feel quite at home, I can assure you."

"The Marski is centrally located?" she asked.

"It is just off Nevsky Prospekt, the city's main thoroughfare, well-placed for visiting the shops, the restaurants and the theatre district."

"Sounds good, Ilya," she remarked. "I intend to take full advantage of my first visit to my grandparents' native country."

"One more matter," he said, "before ringing off. I take it that you insured the sculpture before shipping it?"

"I most certainly did. It is covered by an Italian company called Siccurazione.sa."

"Excellent. Take good care until we next meet." Replacing the receiver, she donned a light jacket and left the hotel in a more settled frame of mind following her conversation with the consular official. Opening her umbrella in the light rain, she proceeded to the bookstore she had espied on a small outlet mall on the edge of town, not a huge distance from Dunes Hotel. She was seeking a reference book on medieval Russian icons, with a view to adding another string to her bow as an investigative journalist. She had read somewhere that, in the newly-affluent sectors of Russian society, very credible fakes were coming onto the market in increasing numbers. With sufficient research, she might be able to do some reporting on the subject for the likes of *Pravda* and *Izvestia*, two prominent Russian broadsheets. It was nearly noon by the time she returned to the hotel with her purchases. She went directly up to her room, packed her valise and descended to the foyer to settle her bill.

*

That same morning, Olivier Breton left his bachelor apartment at Pantin and took the Metro to Gare du Nord, where he had pre-booked a seat on Eurostar. It was a new experience for him travelling by train under the English Channel. Normally, he would have flown to Heathrow, but his superior Louis Dutourd had persuaded him otherwise, claiming that it was quicker by rail, cutting out transfer to Charles de Gaulle airport and checking-in time. It was a popular, speedy service, which landed him at Waterloo International Station around midday.

Yuki Kimura was already waiting, by prior arrangement, at the buffet opposite Platform 9. He recognized her Eurasian features, fringed with dark chin-length hair, from the description Dutourd had given him the previous day. Purchasing a light beer and a ham roll at the self-service counter, he approached her table. She smiled rather shyly at him as he took a seat facing her.

"*Bonjour, Monsieur Breton,*" she said, in a low voice.

"*Bonjour, Mademoiselle Kimura,*" he rejoined.

"I have only little time," she said. "It is my lunch-hour and I must be back at Canary Wharf by one o'clock."

"It is now 12.10 p.m.," Breton said. "You have time. Monsieur Dutourd told me that speak good French."

Yuki wiped her lips with paper tissue on finishing her tuna sandwich, before saying:

"My mother is French. She lives at Rouen."

"And your father?"

"Japanese. They met in Singapore, where they both worked for a leading bank. I was raised bi-lingual, but my first loyalty is to France, where I attended boarding-school just outside Paris."

"Your father is not at Rouen?" he probed.

"My parents divorced two years ago," she replied. "Father returned to Japan, where he runs a business consultancy at Osaka. I have not seen him in over a year. My mother visits London occasionally, mainly for shopping and the theatre. I usually go to Rouen for the holidays."

"And you have this interesting position at Canary Wharf," Olivier Breton remarked.

"I am chief administrative assistant to Matsuo Yamoto, the mission head. He has complete confidence in me and trusts me implicitly."

"What exactly takes place at the Japanese Cultural Mission?"

"We mainly arrange courses in the Japanese language, for Britons in the export business. And in literature for university students, book clubs and adult education purposes. We also do cookery demonstrations and promote tourism. Oh, and we arrange visits by professional troupes from time to time, to present Kabuki and Noh theatre."

The Frenchman took a bite of his roll and a swig of beer, while absorbing this fascinating information.

"Quite a full program," he observed, much impressed. "And you are well-placed to help our cause?"

"I can relay any information I obtain on the movements of special agent Akira Issiguru," she candidly replied. "For security, you had best contact me at home in the evenings by cellphone. This is my number."

She handed him a slip of paper, which he placed in his wallet after a brief perusal.

"Whereabouts do you live, Mademoiselle Kimura, may I ask?"

"I rent a bed sitting-room in the Holland Park area. It is conveniently central, quite cosmopolitan and not too expensive. By the way, you may call me Yuki."

The Frenchman smiled broadly, thinking what an intelligent, attractive and self-confident young person she seemed.

"Olivier," he said, offering a handshake. "Do you have any idea where Akira Issiguru might be right now?"

"It is rather difficult to ascertain his whereabouts at any given moment. I do know that he is tailing an investigative journalist named Vera Weeks, on the assumption that she may lead him to the Zodiac bronze."

"You mean to say that another Zodiac sculpture has genuinely resurfaced?" he asked, in some surprise. "How did the Japanese manage to come by that knowledge?"

"The London correspondent of a Japanese newspaper picked up a rumor about it on the grapevine. Mr. Yamoto thereupon decided to employ Asian students as scouts during the summer vacation. A young man named Keino Sato claimed to have observed the journalist Vera Weeks loading a wooden crate into her car outside an art dealer's at Inversnaid, in the Scottish Highlands. Issiguru was summoned here from Japan, on account of his detailed knowledge of this country and his fluent English. But he has not so far confirmed the existence of the bronze."

"Do you know which of the Zodiac figures it supposedly represents?"

Yuki Kimura shook her head, regretfully.

"All I know," she explained, "is that, of the original twelve bronzes looted by Western troops in the nineteenth century, seven have so far been restored to China."

"Which ones are still missing?"

"Dragon, snake, rooster, goat and dog."

"It will be most interesting to see which of those it turns out to be," Breton said. "What a remarkable sight the complete Zodiac Fountain must have been, as originally conceived."

"I have seen pictures of them online," Yuki said. "I would just love to see the real thing. It must be awesome."

"Take a trip to China," the Frenchman half-seriously suggested.

"I may just do that - one day," she replied, "when I have the time... and the money."

"My brief now," the agent said, "is to claim the new bronze for France. We shall display it, at least temporarily, at the Louvre, to gain maximum publicity before handing it ceremoniously back to the grateful Chinese. My superiors think that will greatly enhance our mutual relationship."

"And I shall do my best to assist you, Olivier," Yuki assured him.

"But you cannot tell me the Japanese agent's current whereabouts?" he remarked.

"He moves around a lot," she informed him. "That is all I know for the moment, except that he recently rented a Volvo C70."

"His cellphone company will inform the Directorate in Paris of the location of his calls," Breton then said. "That information will supplement what you can learn about his movements at Canary Wharf."

"I wish you *bonne chance*, Olivier," she replied, grasping her purse and rising to leave.

"*Merci beaucoup*," he said. "I may need all the luck I can get."

He watched her slim figure negotiate the narrow space between the buffet tables as she exited towards the Underground, before resuming his snack. In a short while, he would ring Dutourd to let him know he had made contact with the mole at Canary Wharf. Interesting, he thought, that the young woman's first loyalties were to France, her adoptive country. The French education system had evidently done a good job in her regard. He fell to musing on his own schooldays at a lycee near Avignon and the trips they had made to watch bullfights in the well-preserved Roman amphitheatre at Nimes, as well as to Marseilles, where they took the boat out to the Chateau d'If, the setting for Alphonse Daudet's *The Count of Monte Christo.*

*

On leaving Lytham St. Anne's, Vera Weeks headed south. It concerned her somewhat, despite Ilya Sorotkin's assurances, that something unexplained had happened at each of her overnight stops after leaving Scotland. As she drove, she reluctantly decided to forego her initial plan of breaking her journey at Manchester, opting instead to continue on to Criccieth, to spend a relaxing couple of days in the cottage Cecil had inherited from his Aunt Mabel. In happier times together, she and Cecil had often spent walking holidays in the unspoiled countryside and bracing sea air of the Lleyn Peninsula, the northern arm of Cardigan Bay. On gaining the M6 motorway near Preston, she put her foot down to reach maximum speed, intent on making good time in order to reach Criccieth by early evening.

She decided to break her journey at Chester, the city closest to the Welsh border. As she proceeded at much-reduced speed along Eastgate, she was conscious of driving on a road first laid down by the Romans in the first century to serve the walled encampment established by a Roman legion under Emperor Vespasian. The walls were still intact, having withstood onslaughts by the Danes and the Normans at different periods. Finding a parking spot near St. John's Cathedral precinct, she alighted and strode in fitful sunshine along Bridge Street. From a previous visit with Cecil, she expected to find a variety of cafes fronting the River Dee. It was just turned one o'clock when she sat down at an outdoor table and ordered a half-pizza with side salad, unaware of an Asian individual clad in a dark business suit reading a newspaper on a bench on the opposite bank of the river. She took her time over her small repast, conscious that she was less than an hour from the Welsh border and the fast dual-carriageway that skirted snow-capped Snowdonia to race down the coast to Caernarvon. As she ate, she observed with interest the motley activity on the river, always a popular venue on a summer afternoon. Young couples in rowing boats, college students in punts and smaller children in pedalloes all took full advantage of the recreational potential of a major river on their doorstep, as it headed in full flow towards the Irish Sea. After a while, she took out the book on Russian icons she had come across that morning at a bookstore in Lytham St. Anne's and perused its contents. On eventually reaching Criccieth in the early evening, she parked her rental car outside the grocery store on the main street of the village and bought the supplies she would need for a short stay. She then eased her vehicle up a narrow dirt road leading to the medieval castle which dominated the scene from its promontory overlooking a bay with sand-and-pebble beaches. A sharp left-hand turn part-way up the slope brought her to Briar Cottage, with its slate roof and overgrown rear garden. Ivy partly covered the gables. She paid scant attention to a dark-blue Volvo, fleetingly glimpsed in her rear mirror as she turned off the main street, focusing instead on opening the windows to air the rooms and on preparing the light meal she would take after her drive down from Chester. Afterwards, she had in mind a stroll along the beach in the evening sunshine, followed by a drink at the local pub, The Porthmadoc Arms, to renew her acquaintance with the friendly locals. She would then hit the sheets, for an early night.

*

On the morning of June 18, Olivier Breton awoke early, to find the sun streaming in through his bedroom window at Castle Hotel, Chester. Cellphone signals the previous day had indicated that Akira Issiguru was in the general vicinity of that city, rich in Roman and medieval remains. On booking in for the night, he had eaten dinner in the hotel restaurant and repaid to the bar for a nightcap before telephoning Yuki Kimura at her Holland Park address. She had informed him that the Japanese special agent had rung Matsuo Yamoto late-afternoon the previous day, shortly before she had left Canary Wharf.

Yuki told him that Issiguru had tracked Vera Weeks to the quaint village of Criccieth, somewhere along the north coast of Wales. The agent had informed the mission head that his quarry had parked her car outside a small cottage, and that he himself would book into Plas Isa Hotel for the night and keep the cottage under close observation the following day, on the off-chance that a large wooden crate would be delivered there. He would dress in hiking gear, to look more like a regular visitor. Since the cottage was situated below what he took to be a main tourist attraction, in the form of battle-scarred Criccieth Castle, his movements should not attract undue attention. Glancing at his Rolex, the Frenchman decided he had an hour or so before breakfast service began. It amused him, as he relaxed between the sheets basking in morning sunlight, to picture a Japanese in English hiking gear attempting to remain inconspicuous in the heart of a small Welsh seaside resort. He would obviously stick out like a sore thumb. When he eventually rose from his bed, he showered and dressed quickly, concealing his pistol in a shoulder holster beneath his leather jerkin. He then went down to the restaurant, chose a table by a window overlooking the River Dee and ordered a full English breakfast. While awaiting service, he again pondered Yuki's information. Did it imply, he wondered, that Issiguru had obtained prior knowledge of the movements of the crate presumed to be holding the Zodiac bronze? Or was he merely assuming that the crate would follow the journalist, and that a Welsh cottage was to be its temporary, perhaps even its final, destination? That struck him as unlikely, as he tucked with good appetite into his mixed grill and served himself a cup of French roast, while watching the boating activity just starting up on the river. One way or the other, he would discover for himself later that day. Rising from his table, he collected his overnight bag, paid his bill and checked out. By one o'clock in the afternoon, he had reached Criccieth, discovering a charming little resort with a village green sloping down towards the sea and a single main street fringed with stone houses and shops. A ruined castle dominated the scene from its grassy promontory. He eased his car along the street until he espied Plas Isa Hotel, one of only two hotels in the village, and drove a short way beyond it before parking. Observing the hotel entrance in his rear-view mirror for several minutes, he saw little sign of activity. The village in general seemed to be in a midday lull, with a mere handful of pedestrians in evidence. He alighted and walked back past the hotel to the dirt road leading up to the castle precincts, where there seemed to be small groups of tourists. Part-way up the slope, he spotted a white cottage with ivy-covered walls. As he crossed to the far side of the street, he suddenly noticed a lone figure descending the slope. Some way behind him was a blue sedan parked at the roadside, whose make he could not immediately discern. As the figure drew nearer, the Frenchman was able to identify him as an Asian dressed in hiking gear, exactly as Yuki Kimura had described. How incongruous that seemed, in the heart of a small Welsh village! He observed the curious individual's progress down the dirt road. When he suddenly opened the gate leading into the cottage garden, Olivier Breton's heart beat faster and he fingered the pistol butt beneath his jerkin, in the sudden awareness that he was observing Akira Issiguru. Re-crossing the street, he turned up the dirt road to assess the situation at closer quarters. As he did so, he heard the sound of a car's horn immediately behind him. Stepping aside to allow the vehicle to pass, he noticed at once that it was a police squad car, which promptly came to a halt outside the cottage. Drawing closer, he observed two men emerge from the vehicle, one of whom was a police officer in uniform. He thought the other man could be a detective. What a striking development, was his instinctive reaction, as he awaited developments.

*

Earlier that day, George Mason had received a telephone call from Cecil Weeks, minutes after his arrival at Scotland Yard.

"Some interesting news for you, Inspector," the musicologist said, excitedly. "I just received an email from Welsh Hydro that the power was switched on at Briar Cottage yesterday afternoon. That can only mean my wife is in residence."

"You and Vera are the only ones who have a key?" an immediately alert George Mason asked.

"That is correct, Inspector."

"So we can assume she is no longer missing? Case solved?"

"I hardly think so, Inspector," came the rather agitated reply. "I need to know why she has not contacted any family member in all this time, and if she is in some kind of difficulty. It did occur to me that she may be held at the cottage under some kind of duress."

"On account of her investigative work?" the detective asked.

"Possibly, Inspector."

The detective pondered the situation for a few moments, aware that he owed it to Cecil Weeks and Irina Carmichael to reach clarification in the matter, even though it now seemed that Vera was no longer missing. The possibility of some sort of duress was a new angle on the case, however, that needed looking into.

"I shall see what I can do, Mr. Weeks," he said. "Where did you say the place was?"

"Briar Cottage is at Criccieth, on the Lleyn Peninsula, North Wales. It is situated on an unmade road leading up to the castle."

"Several hours' drive, in fact?"

"You could be there by early afternoon, Inspector."

"I shall leave at once," the detective assured him. "And I shall call you later today with any news."

"That is very obliging of you, Inspector Mason," the grateful editor replied.

George Mason replaced the receiver and crossed to Chief Inspector Bill Harrington's office to inform him of the new development.

"Better get up there soon as you can, Inspector," Harrington said, "and nail this business once and for all. Enough resources devoted to it already."

"At the very least," Mason said, "it will put the family's mind at rest. And it may lead to some rather interesting revelations about Chinese sculpture."

"What on earth are you talking about, Inspector?" his chief grumpily enquired.

"Vera Weeks was pursuing a rumor that a bronze sculpture looted from the Zodiac Fountain at the Imperial Summer Palace in Beijing has resurfaced."

"Poppycock!" Harrington exclaimed. "Just stick to the facts, Mason, and ignore the rumors. The art world is notorious for its scams."

Feeling somewhat chastened by his superior's remarks, George Mason quickly left the building and descended to the underground parking area. Minutes later, he was negotiating heavy city traffic to reach the M4 motorway, which would take him as far as Bristol. From there, he would cross the Bristol Channel into South Wales, make his way across-country to the coast and follow it to the northern rim of Cardigan Bay. As he left Whitehall, he rang Adele to tell her not to expect him home for dinner.

On reaching Criccieth early in the afternoon, he called first at the local police station, partly as an act of courtesy, partly in case he needed back-up. Sergeant Bryn Williams was surprised to see him.

"What brings the Metropolitan Police to this quiet haven?" he asked, nudging aside the remains of his packed lunch.

"I am here regarding the occupant of Briar Cottage," the detective informed him.

"Cecil Weeks?" the sergeant asked, with some concern. "I know him quite well, even though he rarely visits nowadays. He asked me to keep an eye on the property from time to time. Just routine work in this low-crime area."

"It is his wife Vera I am concerned about," his visitor said. "She has not contacted her family for some time, but I have reason to believe she might be in residence at the cottage right now."

"Is that so?" the local officer asked, evidently surprised. "Then let us go up there straight away and take a look."

Re-buttoning his tunic, he led the way to his car. On parking and approaching the cottage door, they heard voices rising in heated argument within and entered immediately. They found themselves gazing into the barrel of a gun aimed at them by an individual of short stature and Asiatic mien, clad incongruously in hiking gear. The gunman motioned them towards the far side of the room, as he himself stepped backwards towards the part-open door. Vera Weeks was standing by the window, a look of alarm spreading across her intelligent features.

Moments later, the Asian felt the barrel of a revolver between his shoulder blades, as Olivier Breton stepped in from the garden.

"Drop your weapon," he snapped.

Without turning his head, the Japanese agent complied.

"Vera Weeks, I take it," George Mason enquired, addressing the journalist. "What the Dickens is going on here, may I ask?"

"This person here," she replied, indicating the Japanese, "has intruded and he has been harassing me."

"Over a certain bronze sculpture?" the detective asked.

"Who on earth are you?" Vera asked. "And how could you possibly know about such matters?"

"This is Inspector George Mason," Sergeant Bryn Williams explained, "from Scotland Yard."

"I have been trying to track you down for some days," Mason explained. "Your sister Irina and your husband Cecil have been very concerned at not hearing from you."

The journalist sank into a chintz-covered armchair and looked downcast.

"That is unfortunate," she said. "But, in the circumstances, it could not be helped. I did not ring them because phone-calls can be traced."

"What is all this about?" a bemused Sergeant Williams asked.

"Mrs. Weeks has come by an article of considerable value," Mason said, "in the form of a bronze sculpture looted from the Imperial Palace Garden at Beijing in the nineteenth century. Is that not the case, Mrs. Weeks?"

"You seem incredibly well-informed, Inspector Mason," Vera remarked.

"I have reliable sources," Mason replied, matter-of-factly.

"This person here," she continued, indicating the Asian, "entered my cottage uninvited, apparently expecting to discover the bronze, which he evidently wants to acquire, for his own purposes."

All eyes turned towards the intruder, who returned an impassive stare, saying nothing.

"This person is Akira Issiguru," Olivier Breton announced. "He is an agent of the Japanese secret service."

A look of chagrin crossed Issiguru's features. Still silent, he gave an oriental-style bow.

"Cuff him and take him down to the police station, Sergeant," George Mason said. "Charge him with aggravated trespass and harassment."

The local officer did as Mason instructed, leading the handcuffed Japanese out to his car.

"And who might you be?" a much intrigued George Mason asked, addressing the fortuitous new element in the drama.

"Olivier Breton, of the French Directorate," came the assertive reply.

"You are also interested in the bronze?" Vera Weeks pointedly enquired.

"My government has a notable interest in the Zodiac Fountain," he explained. "We returned two of the missing sculptures to the Chinese authorities earlier this year."

"The rat and the rabbit, I do believe," the journalist remarked.

"Quite so," the Frenchman replied. "And we should be most interested in returning a third bronze."

"Which evidently accounts for your presence, too, here in Criccieth?" George Mason enquired.

Olivier Breton nodded, while Vera Weeks merely looked bemused.

"It beats me," she said, "how three different people, from three different countries, have managed to track my movements, when I have taken all possible steps to conceal them."

"Because you have your own agenda regarding the bronze, isn't that so, Mrs. Weeks?" Mason probingly asked her.

"I think we could all use a strong cup of tea," she evasively replied. "Please sit down while I make a brew. Then we can have a thorough discussion of this whole business."

With that, she retreated to the small kitchen at the rear of the cottage and put the kettle on. George Mason and Olivier Breton sat down at the bare dining table and eyed each other cautiously, saying little. Within minutes, the hostess returned and served tea with arrowroot biscuits.

"So a third bronze sculpture has genuinely resurfaced?" the French agent remarked. "I am very gratified to learn that the rumor is true. Which of the figures is it, may I ask?"

"The dog," the journalist replied.

"Wonderful," the Frenchman said.

"So you have been acting purely on supposition, Monsieur Breton?" an intrigued George Mason asked.

"We heard rumors," the other replied. "And it was just too big a thing to ignore. Having learned of the Japanese interest in it, we were doubly motivated."

"So you traced Issiguru – if that is his real name – all the way here?"

"It is Akira Issiguru all right," Breton informed them. "He is temporarily attached to the Japanese Cultural Mission at Canary Wharf, London."

Vera Weeks poured the tea and offered biscuits. They occupied themselves in this quasi-oriental ritual for a few minutes.

"Where is the dog now, Mrs. Weeks?" George Mason wanted to know.

"It is on its way to Cardiff," she informed him. "I shipped it with National Freight Services from Glasgow on June 16."

"When is it due to arrive?" Olivier Breton was interested to learn.

"It should reach Elizabeth Dock around noon tomorrow," the journalist replied. "I have acquired it, after considerable effort, on behalf of the Russian government."

"It truly amazes me," George Mason remarked, "that three totally different countries wish to acquire this single piece of sculpture."

"It is a very significant and valuable object," the French agent said, "whose rightful place can only be at the Louvre, pending future negotiations with the Chinese."

"Which raises a rather interesting question," Mason remarked.

The other two glanced at him expectantly, and a little warily, waiting for an explanation.

"The question," the detective rather officiously continued, "is whether an object of such value, as you both claim it to be, can leave Britain without official export clearance."

"There cannot be any delay," an immediately alarmed Vera Weeks objected. "The crate is scheduled to be loaded onto a Svezda Lines freighter as soon as it reaches Elizabeth Dock."

George Mason, thankful for the modest refreshment after his long drive, sipped his tea pensively. A slew of considerations had now, unexpectedly, been raised. Two foreign agents were on British soil and there was an almost priceless objet d'art to reckon with. He took out his cellphone and dialed.

"What are you doing now, Inspector?" a concerned Vera Weeks challenged.

"I am contacting the Foreign Office," he curtly replied, "by your leave."

The journalist, with a scowl, rose and paced the room nervously. Olivier Breton looked on, much intrigued at the Scotland Yard man's latest move. As the call went through, a senior civil servant came on the line.

"Inspector George Mason here," the detective announced, "from the Metropolitan Police."

"Good afternoon, Inspector Mason," came the reply. "Andrew Forshaw here. What is the reason for your call?"

"Are you familiar with the Zodiac Fountain, Mr. Forshaw?"

There was a pause, before the official replied.

"I seem to recall," he said, moments later, "that earlier this year two missing animal bronzes were returned to China by the French authorities. Is that what you are referring to, Inspector?"

"Indeed, I am," Mason replied. "It now seems that a third bronze sculpture has come to light, somewhere in Scotland, I believe."

"And where is the piece now?"

"It is apparently on its way to Elizabeth Dock, Cardiff, where it is scheduled to be shipped aboard a freighter bound for Russia around midday tomorrow. I am wondering if there is an official view on that."

There was another quite long pause, before Andrew Forshaw said: "An interesting situation, Inspector Mason, to say the least. I shall need to consult with the Foreign Secretary himself, Sir David Finch. He is currently at a meeting in Paris and won't be back at Whitehall until tomorrow morning."

"Will you be able to call me before, say, 10 a.m. tomorrow?" the detective asked, estimating about two hours traveling time to Cardiff.

"Not a problem, Inspector. Sir David should be at his desk by nine o'clock."

Concluding the call, George Mason turned to the other two occupants of the room. Vera Weeks, meanwhile, had resumed her place at table, sitting tensely on the edge of her chair.

"We shall have to wait until tomorrow morning," the detective informed them, "for a definitive view from the ministry."

"The sculpture is now Russian property," the journalist insisted. "It was they who funded the purchase, by transfer to my bank account."

"There is still the small matter of official clearance, Vera," Mason said, with heavy emphasis, now realizing how she had funded the purchase.

At that point, the Frenchman rose to his feet with an air of resignation.

"Now that matters have progressed this far," he announced, "I shall withdraw and return to Paris, to confer with my superior, Monsieur Dutourd. The fate of the bronze will evidently now be decided at government level. Our Ministere des Affaires Etrangeres will contact the British Foreign Office, to press the case for France."

"A rather weak case, Monsieur Breton," Vera Weeks declared, "if I may say so."

"You are entitled to your view," the Frenchman coolly retorted. He then gave a rather enigmatic smile, bowed slightly to each of them and made his exit through the rear door into the rambling garden.

George Mason was left in the company of the investigative journalist, who seemed very put out at this turn of events.

"It will ruin my plans," she complained, "if the bronze does not reach Russia as planned."

The detective returned a sympathetic, questioning look.

"What plans are they, Mrs. Weeks, might I ask?"

"I was invited by the Russian Ministry of Culture to give a series of lectures on Oriental art in St. Petersburg, to coincide with the arrival of the Zodiac bronze. There was to be an official reception, speeches, television interviews and newspaper reports. Now all of this is in the air."

"Perhaps the Foreign Office will be able to work something out with the Russian Embassy," the detective helpfully suggested.

"The French, as members of the European Union, will probably mount a stronger claim," Vera said, resignedly.

"We shall see, Mrs. Weeks. Tomorrow morning, I shall drive down to Cardiff after hearing back from Andrew Forshaw. No doubt, I shall meet you again, at Elizabeth Dock."

"I shall be there without question," she replied. "The Russian Consul will also be present."

George Mason was left musing on the implications of her parting remark as he left Briar Cottage and walked back to the police station to check on the Japanese agent and retrieve his own car. On satisfying himself that Akira Issiguru was, for the time being, safely behind bars, he drove the short distance to Plas Isa Hotel and booked in for the night. He rang Adele to let her know of his change of plan.

"Too bad you can't make it back this evening, George," she said.

"It would be a long trip," he replied. "More to the point, I have to go down to Cardiff first thing tomorrow morning on urgent business. Since I am practically on the doorstep, it will make for a much easier drive if I go from here. Expect me back for dinner around six tomorrow evening."

"Do take care, George," Adele said, as he ended the call.

Since he now had some free time, he took the opportunity to explore his surroundings, after a cheese sandwich and a pint of local ale at Porthmadoc Arms. He took a long walk along the beach, reminding himself of his one previous visit to this part of Wales as a child. How familiar it soon began to seem. His parents often chose the Welsh coast for annual vacations, opting mostly for the busier and livelier resorts of Llandudno and Conwy, where he liked to go crab-fishing using a line baited with bacon rind saved from the breakfast table. Boyhood, he mused! How long ago was that?

Having stretched his legs and enjoyed the sea air, he returned to his room overlooking Cardigan Bay. After catching up on some documents Bill Harrington had left with him to peruse, about another complex case, he dozed off until dinner. On waking, he freshened up and went down to the restaurant, which was about half-full. Having eaten little all day, he tackled one of the hotel's specialties, cod Molly Malone, with good appetite, helping it down with a glass of Soave. Figuring that Irina Carmichael would be at home in the evening, he gave her a call.

"Inspector Mason!" she exclaimed. "I am so pleased to hear from you again."

"Good evening, Irina," he replied. "I have news for you."

"You have found Vera?" she asked, with baited breath.

"Indeed I have. She is safe and well at Briar Cottage, Criccieth."

"I am so relieved to hear that, Inspector," she replied. "Cecil rang me earlier to say that the power had gone on at the cottage, and that you were on your way there. I have been expecting to hear from you."

"I got there in the nick of time, Irina, with Sergeant Bryn Williams, of the local police. He apprehended a Japanese agent who was also at the cottage."

"What on earth was such a person doing there?" an astonished Irina Carmichael asked.

"This whole episode with your sister seems to hang on a Chinese sculpture," the detective explained. "It seems she acquired it at Inversnaid, on behalf of the Russians, and is due to ship it out of Cardiff around noon tomorrow. The Japanese also have their own designs on the same piece."

"You amaze me, Inspector Mason," Irina said. "But why hasn't Vera been in touch with either of us all this time?"

"Because the transfer of the sculpture to the freighter *Svoboda* was to be a highly-secretive operation. Vera was afraid that, if she used her cellphone, her movements and whereabouts at any given moment would be discovered, compromising her mission."

"That is all very puzzling to me," came the reply. "But I suppose it made sense to Vera."

"Were you aware that your sister was planning to visit St. Petersburg?" he then asked.

"Absolutely not, Inspector. That is certainly news to me."

"I have the impression – though she did not say as much – that she was going to accompany the item aboard the freighter and present a series of lectures at St. Petersburg soon after her arrival."

"That must have been arranged at relatively short notice," Irina considered. "Vera would certainly have mentioned it, otherwise."

"Her editor, Auberon Maclintock, did not seem to be aware of it, either."

"How odd is that!" came the reply. "So what are my sister's plans, now that you have intervened?"

"We are both driving down to Cardiff tomorrow morning," the detective said, "to await delivery of the bronze by National Freight Services. We shall take things from there."

"I will call her straight away at the cottage," Irina said. "Now that her agenda is no longer a secret, I do not suppose she would mind filling me in a little. I shall also ring Cecil, to set his mind at rest."

"Probably a good idea, Irina," he agreed, ringing off.

CHAPTER 7

At 9.15 a.m. the following morning, after an ample breakfast in the hotel restaurant, George Mason phoned Bill Harrington, while waiting to hear back from the Foreign Office. The chief inspector was most interested to hear that, despite his initial skepticism, an artifact named the Zodiac bronze really did exist and that it was on its way to South Wales. He was even more interested to learn that two foreign agents, a Japanese and a Frenchman, were also after the piece, commending his caller for his prompt action regarding Akira Issiguru.

"Quite a kettle of fish you've got up there, Mason," he said. "How do you intend to proceed?"

"I am expecting any minute now to hear back from Andrew Forshaw at the Foreign Office, whom I contacted yesterday afternoon," Mason replied. "In any event, I shall be driving down to Cardiff this morning. Vera Weeks and the Russian Consul will meet me there, at Elizabeth Dock."

"Russian Consul, Inspector?" Harrington asked, in some astonishment. "Now don't you start getting in over your head. Ring me from Cardiff, if problems arise. The last thing we want is a diplomatic incident!"

"Will do, Chief Inspector," Mason assured him. "And, by the way, can you get some background information meanwhile on Vera Weeks?"

"I shall send Detective Sergeant Aubrey over to Somerset House," Harrington promised, "and see what vital statistics they have on her. Birth and marriage records, for example."

"I should be much obliged, Chief Inspector."

It was almost ten o'clock when Andrew Forshaw rang.

"I just now spoke with Sir David," he said. "The Foreign Secretary is of the opinion that the Zodiac bronze should by no means leave this country without an export license. The Russian Embassy will need to apply for one through official channels. Even then, there is no guarantee it will be granted."

"Why is that?" the detective enquired.

"On account of the Chinese," Forshaw replied. "This is an extremely sensitive matter, Inspector Mason. Sir David wants at all costs to avoid difficulties with the Chinese, in view of delicate trade negotiations scheduled early next month, including the possibility of their investing in our high-speed rail system."

"I also recently read something about exporting pigs' trotters," Mason said, smiling to himself.

"A multi-million pound deal is in the offing," the official replied, in neutral tones. "Trotters are, in point of fact, considered a delicacy on high-end Chinese tables."

"Good news for our pig farmers, certainly. More to the point, Mr. Forshaw, how should I proceed on my arrival at Elizabeth Dock?"

"You are to contact the local police and have them impound the sculpture. The Foreign Office will authenticate it and reach a decision as to its final destination. These matters are never very straightforward, Inspector. Take the Elgin Marbles, for example. Greece has long been agitating for their return to the Parthenon, but they are still at the British Museum, two centuries after they left Greece."

"Sounds reasonable," George Mason said, foreseeing an interesting situation developing at Cardiff. "And what about Akira Issiguru, currently in a jail cell here in Criccieth?"

"Again," Forshaw replied, "the priority is to avoid diplomatic complications. Since he did not actually harm the Weeks woman, get the local police to drop all charges. I feel sure that Mrs. Weeks will understand our position. The Home Office will then declare him persona non grata and deport him."

"Many thanks for your advice, Mr. Forshaw," Mason said. "I shall act on it."

With that, he replaced the receiver, collected his valise and checked out of Plas Isa Hotel. He called first at the police station to notify Sergeant Williams of the Foreign Office's decision, before heading south through Brecon Beacons on his way to the Welsh capital.

*

Earlier that same day, Rory MacTaggart closed his studio at Back Brae, Tobermory and drove down to Craignure to catch the morning ferry to Oban. From there, he followed a route along Scotland's south-west coast to Stranraer. Parking his car at the harbor, he boarded the midday ferry service across the Irish Sea to Larne. He was in an upbeat frame of mind, reflecting on events of the past few days while enjoying a snack of Arbroath smokies and a glass of McEwen's ale in the self-service restaurant. Smoked haddock and smoked herring, especially in their Scottish guise, were among his favorite foods.

Two days ago, he had also crossed to the mainland from the Isle of Mull, to deliver two new watercolors of the island of Iona to Arklet Studio. On arrival at Inversnaid, he had been gratified to learn that one of his original paintings, a view of Tobermory harbor, had fetched a good price from a Canadian buyer. In the course of his visit, he noted that a certain bronze sculpture he had seen on a previous visit was no longer on display.

Being more preoccupied with paintings, whether in watercolors or oil, it was not something he had closely examined, merely noting that it was a striking effigy of a dog. He had remarked on its absence, drawing the comment from the proprietor that her assistant had crated it for shipping. He had not asked what price it fetched, nor did she volunteer that information. Dealers were often cagey about financial matters, especially if they wished to conceal income from the tax authorities. Items were therefore quite often sold by private arrangement, for hard cash which may or may not go through the books.

He had been more interested, in fact, in the purchaser than in the price. When informed that it was an Englishwoman who seemed very knowledgeable about art in general, he had asked for a description. It tallied with his impression of the intrusive journalist who had had the gall to come all the way to Back Brae to confront him about suspected forgeries. He had soon shown her the door, only to be surprised a few days later by the arrival of her sister and a detective from Scotland Yard! Thank goodness, he reflected, that they had little interest in art, whether genuine or fake, being wholly concerned with the current whereabouts of the journalist. Forging old masters could take a back seat for now, since sales of his authentic watercolors were picking up, not only at Arklet Studio, but also at small galleries on Mull and as far away as Aberdeen and Inverness. It was peak tourist season, which he had carefully prepared for over the winter months. Nudging his finished plate aside, he replenished his beer glass before going out on deck to enjoy the ocean breeze. In a little over an hour he would be in Ireland, where he would take the express train to Cork, on the southern tip of the Irish Republic.

*

Olivier Breton arrived by Eurostar at Gare du Nord, Paris, where he took the Metro to St. Germain-des-Pres. On reaching the headquarters of the Directorate, he sought out Louis Dutourd, who was just concluding a meeting of senior staff. The two repaired to the director's private office, where coffee with croissants was served.

"So you failed in your mission to secure the Zodiac bronze?" Dutourd rather irritably enquired.

Breton gave a helpless gesture.

"There was little I could do, in the circumstances," he said. "We were correct in focusing on the Japanese agent, Akira Issiguru. And we have established that the rumor was true that a new bronze sculpture has in fact resurfaced."

"So what went wrong, Olivier?"

"With Yuki Kimura's valuable assistance, I tracked Issiguru to a small cottage in the North Wales village of Criccieth. Just before I arrived, a C.I.D. officer and a local police sergeant entered the building. I followed them soon afterwards."

"With what result, Olivier?" the director enquired, skeptically.

"I was able to surprise the Japanese, who was pointing a gun at the other occupants of the cottage. He released his firearm and was promptly arrested for trespass and harassment of the occupant of the cottage."

"Who was?"

"An individual named Vera Weeks. It seems that she had acquired the bronze some days earlier – she did not say where – and that it was on its way to Elizabeth Dock, Cardiff. From there, it would be placed aboard a Russian freighter around noon today."

"You mean to say that Russia is to be its final destination?" an incredulous Louis Dutourd asked.

"That would seem to be the plan, at the moment," Olivier Breton confirmed.

The director rose from his chair and paced the room in some agitation.

"We cannot allow that to happen," he declared, on regaining his seat and pouring fresh coffee. "It is of paramount importance that the new bronze should reside for a while at the Louvre, and that we should in due course make a very public show of returning it to China."

Breton, who had not yet had breakfast, helped himself liberally to the refreshments provided.

"What options do we now have, Monsieur le Directeur?" he asked.

Louis Dutourd knit his brow.

"We can attempt negotiations at an official level," he thoughtfully replied. "I shall inform the foreign minister of the situation immediately."

"Do we not also need a back-up plan," Breton asked, "in case diplomacy does not produce the desired result?"

"What sort of thing do you have in mind, Olivier?" the director asked.

"We know the route the bronze will follow," the other said. "The freighter *Svoboda*, of Svezda Lines, will leave Cardiff bound for St. Petersburg. We could ascertain its ports of call en route, board it at night and remove the bronze."

"A daring commando raid?" an immediately intrigued Dutourd said, with an ironic smile. "But it could not be identified as a French operation. That would create an international incident."

"We could take care of that with a multi-ethnic force, out of uniform."

"Drawn from the Foreign Legion, perhaps. An interesting proposition, Olivier. But we have so little time, if the sculpture is due to leave today."

"I have my doubts about that," Breton replied. "The C.I.D. officer at Criccieth implied that an export license may be required before it leaves Britain. That will draw the British authorities into the game. They may develop ideas of their own regarding its eventual destination."

"The British Museum?"

Breton gave a wry smile.

"Very possibly," he replied. "Which gives us time to draw up plans in case the Russians eventually prevail, assuming they use the same shipping line."

"Diplomatic channels seem the best bet for now," Dutourd considered. "But we shall also ask the military to draw up contingency preparations. Leave that little matter with me, for the time being, Olivier. Take the remainder of the day off and catch up on some rest."

Olivier Breton thanked the director for that sentiment, drained his cup and left the Directorate forthwith to catch the Metro to Pantin, feeling more concerned about his live parrot Asterix at that moment, than about a bronze effigy of a dog.

*

When George Mason reached Elizabeth Dock late-morning, Vera Weeks was already there, standing expectantly on the quay with a younger person Mason took to be the Russian Consul. They approached him as he alighted from his car.

"Inspector Mason," Vera said, "this is Ilya Sorotkin, from the Russian Consulate. Ilya, this is George Mason, from Scotland Yard."

The two men acknowledged each other, without shaking hands.

"We regard the Zodiac bronze as the property of the Russian government," the consul bluntly announced.

The detective made no immediate reply. A ship's siren sounded, directing the trio's gaze out towards the bay. A large freighter flying the Russian flag was slowly nearing the dock. They watched it eventually ease into its berth and cut engines. Sorotkin turned towards George Mason, expecting a reply.

"There is the small matter of export clearance," the detective told him. "The Foreign Office informed me only this morning that an artifact of such provenance as a Zodiac Fountain bronze must be thoroughly authenticated by experts from the British Museum and receive official clearance before it can leave the United Kingdom."

Vera Weeks and the consul looked aghast at that remark.

"Such bureaucratic rigmarole cannot be necessary," Sorotkin protested. "The authenticity of the bronze is already established as forming part of the estate of the great-grandson of Colonel Iain Hamilton. The officer and his regiment saw action in the Opium Wars and, more than likely, took part in the looting of the Imperial Summer Palace at Beijing."

Mason inwardly conceded the point, without admitting as much.

"My instructions are to impound the sculpture the moment it arrives by freight."

"In that case," an aggrieved-looking Ilya Sorotkin said, "my embassy in London will make representations to the British Government."

"That is certainly your prerogative," George Mason allowed.

Moments later, a squad car of Cardiff City Police sped onto the dock. Three uniformed officers stepped out, joining the original trio just as a large truck hove into view. It came to a halt alongside the ship. Its driver climbed down from the cab and approached gingerly. George Mason sensed from the look on the driver's face that something was amiss. He looked pointedly at him.

"I am afraid my truck was broken into at the Manchester depot last night," the man explained. "The only items taken were a wooden crate to be unloaded here at Elizabeth Dock and several bottles from a consignment of single-malt whisky from Oban Distillery."

"A crate shipped in the name of Vera Weeks?" the detective asked.

"I do believe so," came the concerned reply. "I have the paperwork in my cab."

Vera Weeks and Ilya Sorotkin, beside themselves with angst, could hardly believe their ears.

"How is that possible?" the investigative journalist heatedly enquired. "Do you not have adequate security?"

"The night watchman at the depot was overpowered by a group of men wearing ski-masks," the truck driver explained.

"No indication as to who those individuals might be, I suppose?" Mason tentatively asked.

"The watchman, Tom Greaves, thought he heard Irish accents. That is all I can tell you, I am afraid."

The detective next turned to the Cardiff policemen, who were standing over to one side, looking redundant.

"Your presence here will not be necessary, after all," he explained. "There is no shipment to impound. It has apparently been stolen en route."

The police trio exchanged looks of amused surprise and saluted the Scotland Yard man, before getting back into their vehicle and speeding away from the dock. Vera Weeks was crestfallen.

"Do you still intend to board the *Svoboda*?" the consul asked her.

"I have no alternative," she replied, with resignation, "to travelling without the bronze. The lecture series is already booked and I should hate to disappoint the St. Petersburg public."

"I shall telephone ahead," the consul said, "to say that there has been some delay regarding shipment of the bronze. It may be that the item will be quickly recovered, in which case we can send it post haste by air freight."

That helpful suggestion seemed to partly mollify the journalist, who strolled to her car to retrieve her luggage from the trunk. Turning towards George Mason before boarding the ship, she said:

"Please explain to Irina and Cecil the reasons for my silence over the last couple of weeks. I am sure you yourself can appreciate the absolute secrecy required in a venture of this type."

"I surely can, Mrs. Weeks," the detective replied, with some sympathy. "If not everybody and his brother, at least the Japanese and the French, for whatever reason, seem to have a keen interest in bronze sculptures."

"I can think of reasons," Vera remarked, without elaborating.

The Scotland Yard detective was left scratching his head at that cryptic remark, as the consul said to her:

"I shall detail someone from the Consulate to drive your car to our garage for the duration of your stay in St. Petersburg."

The journalist thanked him for that, handed him he car keys and bade both men good-bye. Within minutes, she was aboard the freighter, effusively greeted by the captain. The consul gave her a final wave and turned to the detective.

"We shall have to leave this matter in police hands, for the time being, Inspector," he said. "Such a notable object is bound to turn up fairly quickly, in my view. Please contact me immediately in that event, so that we can make the necessary representations in official quarters."

"I can certainly do that much for you, Mr. Sorotkin," George Mason assured him.

As the Russian climbed back into his car, a Chaika sedan imported from Russia, Mason rang Bill Harrington at Scotland Yard to bring him up-to-date.

"So the goods have vanished," the chief inspector remarked, with heavy irony.

"The bronze disappeared overnight from the National Freight Services depot at Manchester," Mason explained. "The only lead we have so far is broad Irish accents."

"Nothing else was stolen?" Harrington asked.

"A few bottles of the Oban single malt, Chief Inspector."

Mason heard a loud groan over the line.

"A fine tipple, Inspector," Harrington remarked. "The thieves evidently have good taste."

"I could have fetched you a bottle on my way through Oban," Mason said, "if I had known you were partial to it."

"You could have," came the rather ironic reply, "if you had thought about it. As it happens, Inspector, I am quite well-stocked for the time being with the Glen Garioch."

"I recall that you visited their distillery near Aberdeen," Mason said.

"About twelve months ago," the other said. "A very worthwhile trip, combined with a tour of the Cairngorms. Wonderful motoring country. But to get back on track, where is the Weeks woman at this moment?"

"She has just boarded a Russian freighter bound for St. Petersburg, where she is to give a series of lectures that were arranged to coincide with the arrival of the Zodiac bronze. She is going ahead anyway, at the behest of the Russian consul."

"We did check out her background at Somerset House," Harrington then said. "It seems that her maiden name was Semyonova. Her parents moved here from Paris and applied for British citizenship after World War 11."

"Her parents, in turn, were probably children of White Russians who fled the Bolshevik Revolution," George Mason suggested.

"Which might account for her strong Russian sympathies, Inspector."

George Mason thought about that for a few moments.

"Do you think, Chief Inspector," he said, eventually, "that Vera Weeks could be an agent of the F.S.B?"

"The successor to the K.G.B.?" a much intrigued Bill Harrington returned. "It is certainly worth considering. I shall contact M.I.5 to check if they have anything on her. There are at any given moment, believe it or not, scores of minor foreign agents operating in London. They feed back information from time to time to their respective governments. Anything at all they consider might be useful."

"You mean industrial and commercial material, rather than military?"

"Usually, Mason," his senior explained, "it is a low-key form of economic espionage, plus items that do not necessarily attract much media attention, such as routine government legislation."

"But spiriting a Chinese bronze out of this country amounts to more than that," Mason proposed. "What could be her motive, if she is working for Russian intelligence?"

"Hard to say at this stage, Inspector," Harrington replied. "As I said, I shall get in touch with M.I.5 and see what their view is. Meanwhile, you are to stay on this case, which may have significant political implications. What we must avoid above all are diplomatic complications"

"The one lead we have so far, as I said, is Irish accents."

"Which gives you a start, at any rate. An Irish group called the Erinesi – they model themselves on the Italian mafia, hence their Italianate name – was recently implicated in the theft of rhinoceros horns from natural history museums, for sale on the black market. They fetch huge prices in the Orient. Just a thought, to get you started. Good luck, Inspector!"

"I may well need it," his colleague drily observed. "By the way, in the meantime have someone vet Siccurazione.sa, an insurance company based at Glasgow that insured the crate, in case they have connections with the Mafia."

CHAPTER 8

On arrival at Cork, Rory MacTaggart made his way by pre-arrangement to The Connaught Arms, a popular pub down by the harbor. He found Colm Byrne and Seamus Scallan seated at a corner table drinking pints of draught Guinness.

"Bang on time, Rory," Byrne, the elder of the two Irishmen said, rising to greet him. "What'll you have for tipple?"

"Guinness'll suit me fine, Colm," the Hebridean artist said.

Colm Byrne crossed to the bar, while Seamus Scallan, whom the new arrival had not previously met, appraised the newcomer carefully.

"You secured the bronze?" MacTaggart asked, the moment the elder man set his pint before him and resumed his seat.

"It is in safe storage, for the time being," Byrne assured him. "Thanks for the tip."

"Thought it might interest you," the Scotsman said, "in view of your contacts on the black market."

"We managed to negotiate a successful sale of your latest forgery to a dealer at Antwerp," Scallan said.

"The Rubens pastoral?" a gratified Rory MacTaggart queried.

"A master work, if ever I saw one," the younger man said, passing him a Manila envelope stuffed with banknotes. "Indistinguishable from the original, except to the most practiced eye."

"You have a sure hand and eye, Rory," Colm Byrne remarked, "enabling us to get premium prices for your paintings."

"Can you move the bronze?" the Scotsman asked. "I am aware it is not your usual line of country."

"We shall put out some feelers for starters, before we ship it abroad. I propose a reversal of the usual fee arrangement. 75% of the proceeds for us; 25% for your good self."

"Since you are happy enough with 25% on my forgeries," MacTaggart replied, "that seems fair enough. Did you have much difficulty acquiring the sculpture?"

Colm Byrne shook his head.

"When you rang about it," he informed him, "Colleen Maguire, our contact at the head office of Siccurazione.sa, an insurance company specializing in freighted goods, identified the relevant transport for us. Luckily, we already had men based at Liverpool, only an hour's drive from Manchester. They went over in the small hours, overpowered the night watchman, took the crate by van to Fleetwood and placed it on board a fishing smack. Oh, and by the way, they helped themselves to a few bottles of the Oban single-malt, for good measure."

"Sounds like a successful hit all round," the forger said, contentedly quaffing his Guinness.

"Mighty good whisky," Seamus Scallan said, with a broad grin.

"Now drink up, Rory," Byrne urged, "and we three shall take a stroll down to the harbor."

The Scotsman readily complied, with a few quick gulps. Minutes later, they made their way down to Cork Harbor, where they entered a storage facility. The bronze contours of a dog were barely visible through the slats of the wooden crate.

"Didn't wish to uncrate it," Byrne said. "It is very handy for shipping the way it is. What do you think it might be worth, Rory, from you knowledge of the art market?"

"Couldn't you just loosen a couple of the slats," the other asked, "so I get a closer look?"

Colm Byrne complied with the request, revealing part of the bronze's head.

"Did Colleen Maguire indicate the insurance value?" the forger asked, peering closely at the object.

"Two hundred thousand pounds," came the reply.

"It is a fair piece of work," MacTaggart said. "It caught my eye at Arklet Studio, at Inversnaid. It should realize at least half that amount on the black market."

"Actually," Seamus Scallan put in, "I think its real value may be far higher than that. I read in the newspaper a while ago that bronzes of animal figures were returned to China by the French, after fetching over one million dollars at auction. If this dog effigy belongs in that category, we have a very hot property indeed."

"You must be kidding, Seamus," MacTaggart countered. "It is just something on similar lines. Lots of sculptors do animals, especially dogs and horses."

"But if Seamus *is* correct," the elder man cautioned, "everybody and his brother will be on the look-out for it. Which means we must get it off our hands as quickly as possible. I say we go for half the insured amount."

Colm Byrne and Seamus Scallan glanced at their visitor for approval.

"How soon can you get it out of Ireland?" the Scotsman asked.

"By weekend at the latest, aboard a fishing smack," Scallan replied. "My brother-in-law, Jim O'Connor, trawls the North Sea herring grounds, just off the Belgian coast."

"Then I will go along with your proposal. After all, you are doing the grunt work, and if you're happy with seventy-five thousand pounds for your trouble, so be it. There is no way, to my mind, that it would fetch over a million dollars."

With that, the trio closed up the storage unit and retraced their steps to The Connaught Arms, to seal their pact with another round of Guinness.

*

Akira Issiguru occupied an armchair in the private departure lounge normally reserved for V.I.P.s flying out of Heathrow. Next to him sat two plainclothes officers from the C.I.D., absorbed in crossword puzzles. In just under an hour, the Japanese agent would board the 2.47 p.m. flight to Tokyo, having been declared persona non grata by the Home Office.

Shortly after two o'clock, a figure he immediately recognized entered through the swing doors and strode towards him.

"Honorable friend," Matsuo Yamoto said, in greeting. "How pleased I am to see you!"

Issiguru rose from his chair and returned the greeting, carefully reading the other's face. Words came easily, he mused; perhaps too easily. How pleased could his fellow-countryman really be to meet him, following his signal failure?

"I obtained permission from the Home Secretary," Yamoto explained, "to bid you farewell in person."

"Most obliging of them," the other replied, with heavy irony.

"Very sorry that your mission was so quickly aborted," his visitor continued, switching to his native tongue to prevent eavesdropping by the C.I.D. "How did it go so wrong, Akira?"

The two plainclothes officers glanced up momentarily from their newspapers on hearing a foreign tongue, exchanged bemused smiles and returned to their puzzles.

"Hard to say, Matsuo," the other replied, with an air of resignation. "I did everything by the book, picking up the journalist's trail from your scout Keino Sato and shadowing her, first to Lytham St. Anne's, then to Chester, and finally to what appeared to be a type of vacation property at Criccieth, North Wales. I am absolutely certain that nobody followed my movements."

"Yet everything came unstuck at Criccieth," Yamoto said. "You were arrested there. On what precise grounds?"

"For aggravated trespass and harassment."

"You were fortunate the police did not press charges against you, honored friend."

"They are deporting me instead," came the rueful comment. "Perhaps as well, since it avoids a court case and adverse publicity for Japan."

"The good name of our country must be preserved at all times," Yamoto said. "But I still do not understand how you could have been tracked to North Wales."

"That is a mystery to me also, Matsuo. A detective from Scotland Yard, in company with a local police officer, arrived on the scene shortly after I entered Briar Cottage. What is equally puzzling is that a Frenchman entered soon after them, placing a revolver between my shoulder blades as I was backing towards the door. He knew immediately who I was and spoke my name aloud."

The mission director gasped in astonishment.

"How could he possibly have known that, Akira?"

The agent threw up his hands in despair.

"I suspect he was an agent of the Directorate in Paris," he said. "If he has spent some time in the Far East, we may have come across each other at some point. But I do not recall that we ever crossed swords."

"The disturbing aspect is that he knew you were at that particular location in Criccieth, at that precise time," a concerned Matsuo Yamoto said.

"I can only conclude that the French somehow got wind of my activities, which implies that they are also interested in the Zodiac bronze."

"That figures," the other replied. "Having restored the rat and the rabbit to the Chinese, they would naturally want to follow that up with a third sculpture, if they could come by it. The goodwill engendered would greatly improve their trading prospects in the Far East. Much of Europe has been struggling to emerge from recession in recent years. Exports are increasingly important to them."

Akira Issiguru rose and paced the carpet thoughtfully for a few moments before crossing to the water dispenser for refreshment, his movements carefully observed by the C.I.D. On resuming his seat, he said:

"Could there possibly be a mole at Canary Wharf, Matsuo?"

The director reacted in surprise.

"How could you possibly think such a thing, Akira?" he asked, visibly shaken.

"Put two and two together, Matsuo. Someone must have been aware of my movements in advance. Who else at the Cultural Mission could know the reason for my presence in England?"

The director, sinking into a spare armchair, said nothing for a few moments. From his sedentary position, he eventually said:

"The only other person who was party to our little arrangement was my young personal assistant, Yuki Kimura."

"Then I suggest that you monitor her activities very closely," the special agent said, in ominous tones. "It will not look well for you back home, Matsuo, if you are harboring a spy."

Matsuo Yamoto rose to his feet, indignantly.

"Esteemed friend," he countered, "how could you make such an insinuation? I would trust Yuki with my life."

"Give the matter some thought," the other said, as the two C.I.D. officers rose to their feet to accompany him towards the boarding area. "I shall say nothing back at HQ, until I hear word from you. Our friendship is worth that much."

"One more thing, Akira," Yamoto said, "before you leave. Where is the bronze now?"

"I wish I could answer that question, Matsuo. In the short time I spent alone with the journalist, she denied all knowledge of it. I would have dismissed Keino Sato's account of the crate at Inversnaid had not the Frenchman appeared on the scene. That immediately confirmed to me that the bronze had in fact re-surfaced, but it certainly was not residing at a certain ivy-covered cottage at Criccieth."

An ashen-faced Yamoto thanked him profusely and gave a stiff bow, before watching his friend disappear into the boarding area.

"Give my best regards to your good wife, Fuji," he called after him.

The special agent, however, was already out of earshot.

*

Two weeks later, George Mason arrived mid-morning at Antwerp International Airport, taking the rail connection to Centraal Station. From there he took a taxi to Police Headquarters, where he was shown by the duty constable into the office of Kapitein Aloys Bogaert. The Belgian officer rose to greet him.

"Glad you could make it at such short notice, Inspector Mason," he said.

"Chief Inspector Harrington told me you may have a lead on the stolen bronze," Mason replied, accepting the offer of a seat.

"We may indeed, Inspector," the other said. "On receiving the notice you circulated through Europol, we made certain enquiries. We have reliable contacts in the Belgian underworld, particularly here in an open city like Antwerp."

"Regarding diamond smuggling, for example?" the canny detective prompted.

Kapitein Bogaert smiled at that remark.

"To name just one area of concern," he replied, "among many in this port."

"A fascinating place, if I may say so," Mason said, "which I have not previously visited. On the way from the station, I noted the house where Rubens lived."

"Rubenshuis?" the other said. "Well worth a visit, if time allows. Now about the missing bronze. It is evidently something very special, according to your circular."

"It was apparently looted from the Zodiac Fountain at the Imperial Summer Palace in Beijing."

"That would be during the nineteenth century, I take it?" Bogaert enquired.

"During the Opium Wars," Mason explained, with an air of erudition.

"Most interesting," the other remarked.

"You claim to have located it right here in Antwerp?" Mason optimistically asked.

The kapitein rose from his desk, donned his uniform kepi and led the way out of the building to a waiting car.

"There is a dealer on St. Jakobsmarkt displaying an item closely fitting your detailed description," he informed his visitor.

"You are sure it is an effigy of a dog, Kapitein?"

"Absolutely."

Within minutes, they had negotiated the heavy traffic to pull up outside an antique dealer's premises. On alighting, they were met on the sidewalk by an elderly gentleman wearing a beret and wire-rimmed spectacles.

"Inspector Mason," Bogaert said, "may I introduce you to Professor Jens Cornelius, Dean of Art History at our university? Professor, this is Inspector George Mason, of Scotland Yard."

The two strangers warmly shook hands.

"Pleased to meet you, Inspector," Cornelius said, cordially.

"The professor will assist you, Inspector, while I make a routine visit to the docks in the Schippersqwartier."

With that, the officer returned to his car as the other two entered the store. A bronze effigy of a dog was on prominent display. The academic approached and examined it carefully, while the detective looked on expectantly. The antiquarian dealer hovered in the background, hoping to make a sale. Some minutes later, the professor led George Mason out of the premises and into a coffee house farther down the busy street. Once inside, they occupied a table by the window.

"What is your considered opinion, Professor?" Mason asked.

"I am afraid, Inspector," Cornelius replied, "that it is a forgery. The metal is in too pristine a condition, showing no signs of discoloration that you would expect from a genuine antique. Another indication is the size. I have visited the genuine sculptures on display at Beijing, in the course of my professional studies. This effigy is on a somewhat smaller scale than those."

George Mason felt keen disappointment at the verdict.

"Do you think it may have originated in China?" he asked.

"Quite possibly," the professor returned. "The art market in general is flourishing there, mainly as a result of higher standards of living and the rise of a new prosperous class of citizens. This is a recent development, Inspector Mason. A decade or so ago, there was little interest in genuine antiques. Quite valuable items could change hands for as little as the price of a packet of American cigarettes."

"You truly amaze me," the visiting detective remarked.

"The problem, Inspector," Cornelius continued, "is that demand now outstrips supply, creating a ready market for forgeries. All manner of artifacts are reproduced by very skilled craftsmen, and on a large scale too. Brand-new putative antiques in jade, porcelain or bronze, for example, are coming onto the market."

"What about paintings?" the curious detective enquired.

Jens Cornelius sipped his coffee thoughtfully.

"That may be a different matter," he replied. "Genuine Chinese paintings now fetch over one million dollars at auction. Reproductions of old masters are also acceptable. You must appreciate, Inspector, that the Chinese revere the art produced in previous centuries and seek to emulate it. They are traditionalists, in short, unlike art practitioners in the West, who must keep coming up with something new. Your Tate Modern gallery in London exemplifies this trend."

"So young Chinese artists are trained in the techniques of the old masters?" a fascinated George Mason asked.

"Exactly so, Inspector."

"Which certainly spares them some of the grotesqueries passing for modern art in the West," Mason added.

The academic raised eyebrows at that unexpected remark.

"It is the shock of the new," he replied, with a knowing smile, "that grabs people's attention for a while, before the next fad overtakes it."

At that point, Kapitein Bogaert returned from the Schippersqwartier.

"Missed you at the antique store," he said. "Thought you might be close by."

"It did not take Professor Cornelius very long to dismiss the bronze as a clever forgery," George Mason said.

"Quite a good forgery, too," Cornelius said, "from what I have seen of the genuine article on display at Beijing."

"Sorry you have had a wasted trip, Inspector," Bogaert sympathized. "I wish you better luck next time."

"I imagine I may get a number of false leads," the English officer remarked, "before alighting on the real thing. But it has to be somewhere in Europe. The question is where."

"I wish you good luck, Inspector Mason," the professor said, rising to his feet. "You must excuse me now. I have to give a lecture on the Ming Dynasty just before noon."

"Can I drop you off at the university?" the Belgian officer asked.

"Thank you, no, Kapitein," came the reply. "It is just a short walk from here."

"Then perhaps our English visitor would care for a brief tour of the city and a spot of lunch before heading back to the airport?" Aloys Bogaert suggested, leading the way out of the café as Jens Cornelius strode purposefully along St. Jakobsmarkt.

George Mason readily agreed to that friendly proposal, climbing into the front passenger seat beside his guide. The kapitein drove at moderate speed through the late-morning traffic, taking in the port, the diamond district, Rubenshuis, the cathedral and a few other notable sights, before coming to a halt outside a restaurant with sidewalk tables sporting umbrella shades.

"I shall treat you to one of our national dishes, Inspector," he offered, "to help you on your way. Then I shall drop you off at Centraal Station, for your rail connection back to Brussels."

"Much appreciated," his visitor replied.

"It is a real pleasure for me," Bogaert continued, "to welcome a fellow Europol officer. We do not have all that much personal contact."

"Because so much is done by internet nowadays," Mason agreed, occupying the seat opposite his host at a table set well-back from the traffic.

The Belgian quickly scanned the menu and placed an order with the waitress, leaving his guest in a state of anticipation. Two glasses of Stella Artois soon arrived, followed minutes later by large bowls of what appeared to the visitor to be a rich kind of soup. A plate of dry bread accompanied it.

"A typical Belgian dish," Aloys Bogaert enthusiastically explained. "Bon appetit!"

"What do you call it?" an intrigued George Mason asked.

"*Waterzooi*," came the reply. "It is traditional cuisine from Ghent."

"What exactly is in it?" the skeptical detective asked, noting the pungent odor.

"Chicken, mixed vegetables, cream and eggs," the other informed him, dipping his bread handily into the broth.

Mason, his doubts overcome, followed suit, enjoying the tasty dish while his host mentioned visits he had made to Britain with his wife and two children. They had been particularly fond of the south-west, on camping trips to Devon and Cornwall, near the resort towns of Dartmouth and St. Ives. The visitor, for his part, recalled with pleasure visits to Bruges and Ostend with his wife Adele, inviting the officer to make contact on his next trip to England. He would show him some of the sights of London.

By the time their appetizing meal was finished, followed by a second round of drinks, and Aloys Bogaert had dropped him off at the train station, they were almost like old friends.

The following morning, George Mason reported to Bill Harrington soon after arriving at Scotland Yard.

"So you drew a blank, Inspector?" Harrington drily asked, on hearing Mason's account of his fruitless visit to Antwerp. "Mind you, I cannot say I am very surprised."

"Have any other leads come in from Europol?" Mason asked.

The senior man nodded.

"Something came in while you were away," he informed him. "The German police have identified an object which seems to fit your description at an art gallery in Bonn."

"That was quick," Mason remarked.

"I imagine you will get scores of these leads," the other said, "before you turn up the right one. All of which will occupy valuable police time, which could be better spent tackling problems nearer home."

"I think the Foreign Office wants us to devote some resources to this," Mason said. "If we, rather than the Japanese, the French or the Russians, can return a Zodiac bronze to China, it will help boost our export market."

"Pigs' trotters, Inspector?" Harrington ironically asked.

"A delicacy, so I believe, at high-end Chinese tables."

"You could have fooled me, Inspector. By the way, we had M.I.5 vet the Weeks woman."

"And?"

"She is not known to them as an active agent of the F.S.B. She could, however, in their view, be one of the low-level affiliates of the sort I mentioned to you a short while back. M.I.5 have entered her on their database as a person of interest."

"So she will now be under surveillance?" Mason asked.

"Not close surveillance, Inspector. They will just keep track of her more out-of-the-run activities including, for instance, her current visit to St. Petersburg."

"I spoke with Cecil Weeks about that," Mason said. "She is apparently due to return any day now from her guest lecture tour and resume journalistic assignments for *The Sunday Post*."

"Well and good," the Chief Inspector remarked. "Less for us to concern ourselves with, when she is safely back in harness."

As his morning refreshments had just crossed the office threshold, borne by an attractive female officer, he reached down to his bottom drawer for his stash of Glen Garioch and poured himself a generous tot to chase the freshly-brewed coffee.

"It helps the concentration," he slyly remarked, without offering it across the desk. "Winston Churchill apparently thrived on this stuff while running the government."

George Mason smiled indulgently, aware that it was his senior's single weakness, apart from Dutch half-coronas.

"I shall leave for Bonn first thing tomorrow morning," he said. "In which case, I shall be leaving early today."

"Bon voyage, Inspector," Harrington replied, pouring himself coffee. "And by the way, while you are in Bonn, you might wish to take a look at Beethoven's house. I know your fondness for classical music."

"I may well do that, Chief Inspector, if time allows."

Returning to his own office to clear up loose ends, he received a call from the reception area announcing the arrival of Irina Carmichael. Minutes later, she was standing before him, clad in a light-gray two-piece suit. What was different about her, he decided after a moment's reflection, was a new hair-do.

"I had some business in town," she said. "Thought I would drop in on you, if you can spare the time."

"Publishing business?" the detective asked, recalling that she wrote historical novels.

"In a manner of speaking," she replied. "I am in London to discuss an audio version of one of my novels."

"And what can I do for you?" he asked, offering her a seat.

"I called mainly to thank you for your efforts in tracing Vera, Inspector. Geoffrey and I are very appreciative."

"You had no idea, did you, of her plans to visit Russia?"

"None whatsoever," she replied. "And I am frankly still rather annoyed that she has been so secretive about it."

"It is the nature of the enterprise," Mason said. "Everybody and his brother seems interested in a certain Chinese sculpture. Your sister stole a march on all of them and would have fully succeeded had not the Irish mafia intervened."

"So where is the bronze now, Inspector?"

George Mason simply shrugged.

"Anybody's guess, really, Irina. We have been putting out feelers with Europol, and I am leaving for Bonn first thing tomorrow morning, to follow up a fresh lead."

"You certainly move around, Inspector," Irina said, in complimentary vein. "The Isle of Mull, the Scottish Highlands, the Lleyn Peninsula, Bonn…"

"Antwerp, too, as of yesterday."

"A comprehensive itinerary, Inspector."

There was a pause in the conversation, while the detective framed a more delicate question. Eventually, he said:

"Were you aware, Irina, of Vera's close dealings with the Russians? I know, for instance, that your grandparents were Russian émigrés."

The author returned a look of surprise that he would know something like that.

"In her work as an investigative journalist," she replied, "my sister delved into many areas, not just the art world. She has always had strong Russian sympathies, much more so than I myself. I think she inherited it from her father, who long wished to visit his parents' native land, but he died before the political barriers came down."

A possible connection with the F.S.B came to Mason's mind, but he thought that matter was best left to M.I.5. He doubted that, if his visitor knew of such, she would not be likely to divulge it, to protect her sister, with whom she was evidently very close.

"Have you had recent contact with your sister Vera?" he asked.

"She rang me at home in Christchurch, from the October Hotel in St. Petersburg," Irina replied. "She told me that her series of lectures was now over and that it had been well-received. She should be back home very soon."

"For a happy reunion, no doubt," George Mason genially remarked.

CHAPTER 9

Herman Eades was a large-framed man with a ruddy complexion and thinning blond hair. Now in his early sixties, he had made his fortune mining potash in Arizona, retiring early to concentrate on his growing collection of fine art. At his private gallery in a suburb of Phoenix, he had amassed an assortment of European paintings, particularly of Impressionists and Cubists. Over recent months, he had broadened his purview to accommodate Oriental art, mainly paintings and sculptures, having watched their values steadily rise over the years at prominent auctions. His passion for collecting had come rather late in life, arising from the simple fact that it was something other wealthy people did. Their motivation, he figured, was as much to preserve and increase their wealth, as to appreciate artistic achievement of the highest order. Country club discussions had often turned on the topic of this or that artist currently in vogue, or out of favor. Herman Eades wanted to be part of the conversation, having noted the astronomical prices notable works of art could fetch. Collecting, in short, was a solid form of investment.

Having finished tying up his yacht, the *Teal*, at a berth in Nice harbor, he set about clearing the foredeck of the previous night's accumulated junk, before going below to join his partner for lunch. Nicola Montales had thrown a short floral apron over her sea-blue swim-suit, to set the table for two and prepare a light meal of smoked salmon and avocado, with a fresh baguette. She had first met her companion at an art exhibition in Los Angeles featuring Monet and Pissarro. A mutual interest in the Impressionists formed an immediate rapport between them. The daughter of Mexican immigrants who struggled to maintain a basic standard of living on moving to California, she also viewed Herman as her meal-ticket. The fact that she had taken part-time seminars in art history at UCLA, financed from her earnings as a local tour guide, had spurred the industrialist's interest in her. She could point him in the right direction, he felt, given the pitfalls of the contemporary art market. The last thing he wanted was to be taken as a sucker. Or to become a laughing-stock at the country club.

The simple meal was already laid out by the time he had finished his chores. The previous evening, he and Nicola had hosted a small party for old friends who happened to be passing through Nice following a motoring tour of the Savoy Alps. Empty wine bottles, beer cans and the like had to be cleared away. The deck needed to be swabbed.

"Ship-shape again, Herman?" Nicola asked, as they sat facing each other across the rather cramped formica-topped table.

"Bristol fashion," her companion replied, uncorking a bottle of white wine.

"So what have we planned for today?"

"I think, after lunch, we could take a look round Nice after calling at Tourist Information. We could also visit the art galleries and end up with dinner somewhere. The Reids last night mentioned the Vieux Port as a good place to try. They said it has excellent seafood restaurants."

"Sounds good," Nicola said, taking a sip of the Chardonnay.

"Better slip something on over your bikini," Herman said, "to avoid wowing the natives."

His partner, well-aware that she had a good figure, smiled appreciatively at the perceived compliment, while regarding his remark as unnecessary. Of course, she would slip on a skirt and top before venturing into the well-heeled Mediterranean city.

"Are you looking to make a purchase on this trip, Herman?" she asked.

"It's as well to be on the look-out," he replied. "If we spot something interesting, we may consider it. Not that there is likely to be much in the oriental line here in Nice. Paris, or perhaps even Marseilles, would be a better bet."

"The course I took in Chinese sculpture should come in handy," Nicola said.

"Or Japanese porcelain."

"Exciting, isn't it, Herman, to be involved in the art market?"

"I am devoting my retirement to it," he answered. "I aim to have the best collection of anyone at my country club."

Nicola Montales raised her glass.

"I shall drink to that!" she gaily remarked.

Their meal finished, the skipper went to clean up after his chores and change out of his Bermuda shorts into a pair of white slacks; while his partner added to her brief attire and applied careful make-up. Twenty minutes later, they were strolling along Promenade des Anglais, in strong afternoon sunshine, catching the fresh breeze coming in from the Ligurian Bay, while observing the bathers beneath the swaying palm-trees. Eventually, they located the Office de Tourisme, which produced a daily bulletin of events in the city. Nicola had sufficient grasp of French to decipher it for her companion.

"What treats are they offering today, Nicola?" he asked.

"Quite a variety of activities," came the reply. "Guided kayaking out on the bay, for example, starting at two o'clock."

"A bit too energetic for me," Herman dismissively remarked.

"How about a flower show at the Jardin des Plantes."

"A botanical garden could certainly be interesting," Herman considered.

"There is also a vintage car rally, but that is only for certified owners of suitable vehicles, which effectively rules us out."

"Scrub that."

"A concert of chamber music in the Franciscan monastery garden. How about that, Herman?"

"What is the program?"

"Mozart and Debussy, starting at four o'clock."

"I enjoy the Mozart quartets," her companion said. "Not sure about Debussy. Didn't know he wrote much for strings."

"If I can make a suggestion," Nicola said, "why don't we first visit the flower show and after that find our way to the monastery. By the time the concert is over – probably around six – it will be getting time for dinner."

"A nice al fresco meal in the old port," Herman said. "Sounds good. The Reids raved about the bouillabaisse they serve at the restaurants there. They said that the tables were placed along the quay, so that you could watch the fishing smacks preparing their gear for overnight sailings."

"That would be simply fantastic, Herman," Nicola said, squeezing his arm.

"And tomorrow," he said, "we shall sail down to Monte Carlo and try our luck at the famous casino."

Nicola gave his arm another squeeze, before obtaining directions to Jardin des Plantes and the Franciscan monastery. Whereupon, they set off at a brisk pace to enjoy what the Riviera city had to offer, in addition to sunshine and balmy sea breezes.

*

Chief Inspector Bill Harrington requested a meeting with George Mason, the day after the latter's return from Bonn.

"So you drew another blank?" he asked, with concern.

"Afraid so, Chief Inspector," Mason confessed.

"The Irish police are looking into the matter at their end," the senior officer explained. "They think it very likely the Erinesi are involved, but they have no concrete evidence so far."

"Do we ourselves have anything on the Irish mafia?"

"Nothing beyond cigarette smuggling," Harrington replied. "They have been fairly quiet in London so far this year. Bigger fish to fry elsewhere, perhaps."

"Such as fine art forgeries?"

"What makes you say that, Mason?"

"Vera Weeks seemed convinced that Rory MacTaggart was a forger of old masters. Her sister told me, while we were in Scotland, that Vera was not aware of any network in England to handle them. It occurred to me, since Mull is very close to Eire, that that could be a possible transit route. It is a short sea-crossing."

"I shall mention it to the Garda in Dublin," the other promised. "Meanwhile, I should like you to go to Zurich."

"Another lead?" an alert George Mason asked.

"While you were away in Germany," the other explained, "I received a call from Leutnant Rudi Kubler, of the Zurich Polizei Dienst."

"I know him well," Mason said. "He has helped me on several major cases in recent years."

"It seems that Leutnant Kubler was contacted by a professor from the Academia del' Arte at Bellinzona, wherever that is."

"It is the capital of Ticino," an intrigued George Mason replied. "The Italian-speaking region of Switzerland."

"Which you are more familiar with than I am, Inspector."

George Mason, inwardly gratified at the implied compliment, merely returned a questioning look.

"What is it all about?" he asked.

"Leutnant Kubler did not give any specifics," his chief continued, "beyond saying that the academic had approached him of his own accord. Kubler, having seen your Europol circular, thought what the man had to say might be of interest to Scotland Yard."

"Very thoughtful of the lieutenant," Mason observed.

"Mind you," Harrington continued, "Kubler hastened to add that it may not be quite what you are looking for. Probably just another waste of time, if you ask me, but in view of your past useful liaisons with the Swiss police, I see no harm in your going over there to see what he has to say. You could spend a few of your remaining vacation days there, in case more than one lead turns up. You will then be on the spot."

"I shall gladly do that, Chief Inspector," Mason replied. "Zurich is a kind of crossroads between northern and southern Europe; almost anything can turn up there, especially if big money is involved. Rudi Kubler usually has his finger on the pulse."

"There is a direct flight out of Gatwick tomorrow, at 9.40 a.m. I had a clerk check the schedules. She also booked you a room at Hotel Adler, in the Altstadt."

George Mason returned to his own office in buoyant mood at the prospect of meeting again with a contact who had proved very useful in the past. If it turned out to be another fool's errand, at least it meant that European police forces were acting on his alert. He would spend the remainder of the day writing up reports on Antwerp and Bonn, which were now overdue, and on other routine matters, before leaving Whitehall early, to make preparations for his next trip.

*

"Good to see you again, Inspector," Rudi Kubler said, as George Mason stepped into his office around noon the following day, after transferring by rail from Kloten Airport to Zurich Hauptbahnhof.

"Always a pleasure to revisit your fascinating city," the detective replied, "and to renew acquaintances."

"I booked a table for us at the Wienerwald restaurant fronting the lake," the Swiss officer said. "We can enjoy what you British are apt to call a working lunch."

With that, he led the way to his car, parked at the rear of the Polizei Dienst. A short drive along the Limmatquai and across the busy junction at Belle Vue brought them to the northern shore of the lake, where they parked beneath the spreading chestnut trees and strolled to the popular restaurant.

Kubler suggested schnitzels with side salad for both of them, together with steins of the local Hurlimann's ale. George Mason raised no objection to that.

"What is all this about Zodiac bronzes, Inspector?" the rather bemused lieutenant asked, after placing the order. "I read your Europol circular, but I couldn't make much of it."

"It is a whole new field of enquiry for me, too," his visitor confessed. "It seems that a group of twelve bronze sculptures representing the Chinese Zodiac were looted well over a century ago by French and British troops during the Opium Wars."

"Taken from the Imperial Summer Palace at Beijing?"

George Mason nodded.

"They were displayed round a fountain in the palace courtyard," he explained. "Some of them have been restored to China by the French, but others are still missing."

"Your circular mentioned the effigy of a dog, Inspector."

"Correct, Leutnant," Mason responded. "Did the professor in Ticino mention the same animal?"

"Not in so many words," Kubler said. "But I think it may be worth your while meeting him. I could not persuade him to come up to Zurich to meet you, so the alternative is for you to travel down to Bellinzona, which is about two hours away by train."

"Is the meeting already arranged?" Mason wanted to know.

"I took the liberty of arranging it for you," the other said. "Isidore Scarpa will meet you off the 3.05 p.m. express from Zurich, by which time his duties at Academia del' Arte will be over. He offers extra-curricular courses during the summer months."

"Will I be able to get back to Zurich this evening?

"I see no problem with that," his companion said. "The express from Milan, the *Manzoni*, reaches Bellinzona at 10.13 p.m. You should be back here a little turned midnight."

Their lunch having arrived, they addressed it with good appetite, while observing the busy lunch-hour trade. It was one of Zurich's most popular restaurants, with a view across Lake Zurich towards the snow-capped alps beyond. Tourists mingled with city workers and students from the Polytechnic.

A pianist played a medley of well-known tunes. After the meal, since they had a couple of hours to spare, the detective accompanied Rudi Kubler along the promenade, to view some modern sculptures that had recently been erected on a grassy promontory facing the lake.

If George Mason had been expecting something resembling a Henry Moore or a Barbara Hepworth, he was disappointed. The metal artifacts on display did not strike him as particularly skillful. On eventually returning to the police car, his Swiss counterpart dropped him off at the Hauptbahnhof to catch the Milan express.

"How will Professore Scarpa recognize me?" Mason asked Kubler.

"I gave him a full description," the Swiss replied. "For good measure, fix this pink carnation in your lapel. The academic will be on the look-out for it."

"You think of everything, Leutnant," an appreciative George Mason said.

"Swiss efficiency," the other jocularly replied.

They bade each other a cordial farewell, before Mason entered the station and boarded the train. The *Schnellzug* took him on a scenic route through the northern alps, before entering the seemingly endless Gotthard Tunnel, to emerge into the gentler landscapes of Ticino, before arriving bang on time at Bellinzona. On alighting from the train and walking towards the buffet, the detective soon noticed a casually-dressed elderly man peering quizzically in his direction through wire-rimmed spectacles.

"Inspector Mason?" the man enquired, as he approached.

"The same," George Mason returned.

"Very pleased to meet you, Inspector," he continued. "Leutnant Kubler has given me good reports of your professionalism."

"Very kind of him, I am sure," the detective rather diffidently replied.

"Let me first offer you coffee, after your long trip," Isidore Scarpa then said, leading the way into the self-service buffet. "I could use one too, after a long seminar."

Serving themselves, American-style, from the array of coffee dispensers, they occupied a corner table in the crowded buffet.

"You are no doubt wondering, Inspector," the academic then said, "why I asked you to travel down to Bellinzona?"

"It had crossed my mind, Professor," came the matter-of-fact reply.

"You are interested in the Zodiac bronzes?"

"That is correct."

"A short while ago, while visiting downtown Bellinzona," Scarpa continued, "I saw a notice about a stolen Chinese sculpture in the window of the central police station. It intrigued me at once, in view of my professional interest in Oriental art."

"I issued a circular to Europol," George Mason explained. "The Swiss police must in turn have notified your cantonal authorities."

"You have Leutnant Rudi Kubler to thank for that," the other remarked. "He took the initiative in the matter."

George Mason sipped his French roast, while the academic went to serve himself a Danish pastry.

On returning to the table, the latter said:

"Shortly after reading the police notice, I received out of the blue a telephone call from a certain Li Fournier. He had been watching a program on television about the Zodiac Fountain and he invited me to visit his villa, a few miles north of here, saying that he had something he felt might be of considerable interest to me."

"He has acquired the effigy of the dog?" George Mason optimistically enquired.

Professore Scarpa quickly finished his pastry and nudged his plate aside.

"Fournier did not give me precise details," he replied. "He seemed very cagey, as if afraid there might be some problems with the authorities."

"Because he had learned that the bronzes were looted?"

"Quite possibly, Inspector," the academic replied. "But what he mainly seemed concerned about was having the sculpture authenticated by an expert. That is why he contacted me, at Academia del' Arte."

"And you, in turn, contacted the police?"

"I informed them of Fournier's approach to me. They advised me to appraise the item first, to see if it was genuine. That explains your presence in our historical city, Inspector Mason. You are to accompany me to Villa Serena, at Leutnant Kubler's suggestion."

The detective smiled to himself at the notion of his Swiss counterpart's behind-the-scenes maneuvers.

"We are to go there straight away?" he asked.

"Li Fournier is expecting us this very evening," Scarpa told him.

With that, the academic led the way out of the station to the forecourt, where his vehicle, a Peugeot sedan, was parked. Within minutes, they had cleared the city, following a winding country road through vine-covered hillsides and mellow stone farm buildings in various states of repair.

"What type are these vines?" an interested George Mason asked.

"In this particular area, we grow the traditional varietal," the academic replied. "It is called the Bondola. But the grape predominantly cultivated in Ticino is now the Merlot. They did a major replanting of the vineyards about a hundred years ago, to improve quality. Cabernet Franc is another of our popular varietals."

"I have always enjoyed Italian wines," Mason said. "Soavi, Valpolicella, Chianti and so on. I have never really tried the Swiss vintages."

"We shall try one over dinner later," the other promised, as the Peugeot took a left turn down a winding dirt track, to draw up outside a small villa with faded stucco and a rambling, ovegrown orchard.

They alighted from the vehicle and knocked on the heavy oaken door of Villa Serena. It was opened moments later by a stooping figure somewhat older than the professor. He appraised them cautiously, before admitting them. The front door opened onto an atrium lit by a skylight. The oblique rays of the evening sun cast an eerie glow on a life-like creature rearing up with jaws agape, as if about to strike. George Mason, startled to the core, froze in his tracks.

"The snake!" exclaimed an ecstatic Isidore Scarpa, stepping closer.

Recovering his poise, the detective gingerly followed suit.

"What an incredible find," the academic said, examining it closely.

"Is it an authentic piece?" the detective asked.

"Unquestionably," came the professor's considered reply, after viewing the bronze from all angles.

"How can you be so sure, Professor?" Mason asked.

"I have been to Beijing with the express purpose of studying the Zodiac Fountain figures. My academic specialism is Oriental art, particularly with reference to sculpture and jade porcelain. I have published numerous papers on the subject in learned journals. I would stake my reputation on my assessment of this bronze."

"I accept your opinion, Professor," the fascinated visitor said, himself walking round the sculpture to appreciate its life-like qualities. "It is truly an amazing piece of work."

Li Fournier was evidently well-satisfied with the academic's verdict.

"How did you come by so priceless an object?" Isidore Scarpa asked him.

"It has been in my family for several decades," Fournier replied. "I only began to suspect its true provenance after hearing on a television current affairs program about two Zodiac bronzes returned to China earlier this year by the French authorities. I researched the still-missing figures and discovered that the snake was among them, along with the horse, the dragon, the goat and the dog. Five pieces in all."

"You suspected," George Mason said, "but you needed verification?"

"That is so," came the reply.

"It has been a sort of family heirloom, has it?" Scarpa asked.

"My father acquired it in Saigon," Fournier explained. "He was a colonial servant in French Indo-China after World War 11. My mother was Chinese by birth. They first met in Saigon and were later married at Singapore.

When the French withdrew from Indo-China – Vietnam, as it is now known – they returned to Europe and eventually retired to Ticino, having earlier bought Villa Serena as a vacation property. The snake has stood here in this atrium as long as I can remember. When I was a young child, it quite terrified me, I must admit."

"That is hardly surprising," George Mason said, having recovered from his initial shock.

"What do you propose to do, Signore Fournier," the professor asked, "now that you know this piece is genuine?"

"Come through to the garden and I shall explain. My housekeeper has prepared some light refreshment.

The trio left the house through the rear door, which opened onto a delightful garden with a profusion of summer flowers in bloom and scented overhanging trees. A small glass-topped table had been set with a carafe of white wine, a dish of mixed nuts and a plate of petit-fours. Their host, filling their glasses, invited them to sit.

Isidore Scarpa tasted the wine and said to George Mason:

"This is the Pinot Blanc, Inspector. One of our noted whites, along with Chardonnay and Pinot Gris."

Mason took a sip, sliding it slowly over his palate, before nodding his approval.

"A nice balance, Professore," he remarked, "with citrus and apricot undertones."

The academic was pleased at his reaction.

"This evening," he said, "we shall try the Bondola."

"I hear you are producing good wines now in England, Inspector Mason," Li Fournier remarked.

"Sparkling wines and whites, mainly," the detective replied. "Climate change is pushing viticulture ever farther north. Why, one day I expect they will be producing fine Merlot in Scotland!"

The other two shook with laughter at that remark.

"That is still some way off, I should think," Isidore Scarpa humorously rejoined.

"Let us hope so," their host added. "Although it may eventually become too warm in southern Europe to grow grapes at all."

"Climate change poses many challenges," George Mason said. "The continuing drought in California, for instance, is already causing serious cutbacks in agriculture."

"I have read about that," their host said. "Aquifers are diminishing rapidly and fields are being left fallow, as a consequence."

They addressed the light refreshments for a while in silence, apart from the humming of the bees targeting the honeysuckle, before Isidore Scarpa said:

"What are your plans for the priceless object in your atrium, Signore Fournier?"

"I have given the matter some considerable thought over recent weeks," the other replied, "in case the snake turned out to be genuine. Since it is part of my mother's native patrimony, I have more or less decided to return it to China."

"What about your natural heirs, Signore?"

Li Fournier shook his head, regretfully.

"My wife Mirina and I remained childless," he said. "Mirina passed on just two years ago, so I have no natural heirs. My father Auguste paid good money for it at Saigon, but that does not mean I have a permanent claim on it, since it was originally looted from the Summer Palace. Its legitimate home must be China."

"A courageous decision, Signore Fournier," an impressed Isidore Scarpa concluded.

"Also realistic," came the immediate reply. "What would happen to it when I died? It would only end up in some museum here. Or worse still, in some billionaire's private collection."

"Do you wish us to help you in your objective?" George Mason asked.

"I was hoping, Inspector, that perhaps you could make representations on my behalf to the Chinese authorities. Sound out their reaction. I could easily take care of shipping arrangements and insurance costs."

The detective thought about that. If the offer came through the British Foreign Office, he mused, it would improve Britain's stock with the Chinese, boosting prospects for British exports, whether they be pigs' trotters for high-end tables, Scotch whisky or novel English wines.

"When I return to London tomorrow," he said, "I shall get in touch with the Foreign Secretary, Sir David Finch, and raise the matter with him. You have my assurances on that score, Signore Fournier."

"I am deeply grateful to you, Inspector Mason," their host replied. "And also to you, Professore Scarpa, for sparing me some of your valuable time."

"Do not mention it," the academic hastened to reply. "I should, of course, naturally have wished to see such a fine object, of considerable historical importance, on public display at our national museum. But I fully respect your decision to honor your mother's memory by restoring it to the country of her birth."

"More wine, gentlemen?" a gratified Li Fournier proposed.

A few drinks later, after a last look at the arresting bronze, the two visitors were on their way. The sinking sun cast a reddish glow over the landscape, on the winding road out of the hills towards Bellinzona. Isidore Scarpa again parked his car on the station forecourt, leading Mason on foot to an Italian restaurant, where they dined on veal cutlets with pasta, helped down with a bottle of Bondola from what the professor claimed to be one of Ticino's leading vineyards.

*

Around noon of that same day, Herman Eades finished mooring the *Teal* at a berth inside Monaco harbor, just below the cathedral, before going below deck for the *salade Nicoise* Nicola had prepared for their lunch. After eating, Nicola changed out of her bikini into a blouse and slacks, tied her hair up in a pink chiffon scarf and set out to explore the principality with her partner. Their path took them round a harbor dotted with large ocean-going yachts they paused briefly to admire, before continuing through the elegant downtown area towards the Jardin Exotique, which reminded them of their visit to Jardin des Plantes at Nice. On this occasion, however, they were less interested in formal gardens and exotic flora than in antiques. Herman Eades had not bought anything beyond souvenirs since arriving at Mediterranean resorts days ago.

He was of a mind to add something significant to his private gallery outside Phoenix, before heading out across the Atlantic to Madeira, to stock up on Madeira wines. His guidebook indicated Rue de Molle for art dealers and antiquarians.

On locating it, they visited each venue in turn, viewing their displays of mainly European art, everything from pottery and jewelry to paintings and sculptures. Nicola showed much interest in a Corot landscape. Herman Eades, while allowing that it was a fine piece of work, persuaded her instead to consider the Impressionists. His main focus, however, was something Oriental, having read that Chinese artworks in particular were fetching ever-higher prices at major auction houses.

"Looks like you are going to be out of luck, Herman," Nicola remarked, when they called at a sidewalk café for refreshment, after spending most of the afternoon rummaging through one store after another.

"The stuff they have here in Monaco is of high quality, on the whole," her partner replied. "Considering the *per capita* income hereabouts, that is only to be expected. Millionaires have no time for second or third-tier art."

"But is it much different from what you could find in almost any major European city?" Nicola asked.

"A good point, Nicola," Herman replied. "I am really on the look-out for something really special. Something that cannot fail to impress the most discerning members of my country club."

Nicola smiled to herself, while sipping her drink. The one-upmanship among wealthy members of a country club merely amused her. Having risen from relative poverty, a reasonable standard of living and occasional luxuries, such as this Mediterranean cruise and fashionable clothes, was all that she really aspired to. She did not much care for expensive jewelry, but took care to humor her rather obsessive partner, if he chose to buy her the occasional necklace or bracelet. To some extent she sympathized with his current obsession: it was a big step from potash to fine art.

"I espied in the window of the last store on this street," she said, "what appeared to be a bronze sculpture. Perhaps you should take a look at that, Herman."

"A bronze?" he enquired. "That is something I do not possess at the moment. Nobody at the country club has mentioned bronze sculptures, either."

"You could steal a march on them," Nicola artfully prompted. "It looked very appealing to me. An animal effigy of some kind."

"What a bright girl you are, Nicola," her partner replied, draining his glass of chilled lager. "Let's go take a look."

Easing his large frame from the low chair, he led the way across the narrow Rue de Molle to a store named Chez Alfredo, pausing to glance at the item Nicola had mentioned. Holding a prominent place in the window display, it immediately struck the collector, familiar with catalogs, as having an Oriental cast. The pair ventured inside.

"*Bonsoir, Monsieur et Madame*," the proprietor said, in greeting.

Herman Eades merely nodded in response.

"*Anglais?*" the other asked.

"American," Nicola hastily corrected him.

"How can I assist you?" the owner said, in quite competent English.

"That bronze you have on display," Eades said. "What can you tell me about it?"

"It is a reproduction," came the reply, "of an early Chinese bronze. The asking price is a mere 20,000 euros."

"What type of creature does it represent?" a puzzled Herman Eades said.

"It represents a mongoose, *Monsieur*," came the rather condescending reply.

The yachting pair drew nearer to examine it more closely.

"Interesting lines," Nicola Montales observed, quite taken with it.

"I am really looking for something more authentic," her partner said. "Certainly not a reproduction."

The proprietor weighed up the couple carefully, soon taking them for the wealthier type of Americans, in contrast to the cost-conscious young people who often visited his store during the summer months, to browse rather than to buy.

"I can put you in touch with a very rare antique," he said, confidingly.

"And what might that be?" a dubious Herman Eades asked.

"My brother-in-law, Vittorio Rossi, told me that he has recently acquired a bronze figure from the Zodiac Fountain at Beijing."

"What the Dickens is that?" Herman Eades challenged, never having taken horoscopes and the like very seriously.

"The Zodiac Fountain was a prominent feature of the Imperial Summer Palace at Beijing," Alfredo explained. "It consists of twelve bronze figures representing the Chinese Zodiac. They very rarely come onto the market, and their prices are always high."

The potash mogul was immediately intrigued.

"Give me a ballpark figure," he said at once.

"Vittorio is asking one million euros for it. It is the opportunity of a lifetime, *Monsieur*."

Herman and Nicola exchanged quizzical glances.

"We could certainly view it," Eades said. "Is your relative's store nearby?"

Alberto smilingly shook his head.

"I am afraid not," he replied. "He lives farther down the coast, at San Remo, on the Italian Riviera. There is a regular bus and rail service from Monaco."

"Does it have a good harbor?" the practical Nicola asked.

"Without question. If you are sailing, you can be there in half a day."

"Vittorio's address?" Eades quickly asked.

"His business is named Antichita di San Remo, on Via Padre Antonio."

"Give him a call," the American replied, "and have him hold it until we arrive there tomorrow. We are definitely interested."

"Vittorio will be most willing to oblige you," the dealer said, "especially if the request comes from this quarter."

That settled, the yachting pair left the store and retraced their steps to the harbor.

"What a turn-up, Nicola," Herman said. "A valuable Chinese antique!"

"They will be green with envy at the country club," Nicola said, giving his arm an affectionate squeeze.

"Let us not get ahead of ourselves, Nicola," her partner warned. "We have not even seen it yet."

"I feel sure, Herman, that you will like it well enough," she replied. "And you can easily afford it."

On retracing their steps back towards the harbor, they passed the imposing city theatre, noting with interest that a touring Japanese troupe were in residence. Nicola paused for a few moments to look at stills showing the elaborate costumes the actors wore for the performance of traditional theatre called Noh. Her partner, less interested, strolled on ahead.

Nicola caught up with him as he reached the *Teal*, going at once to her own cabin to rest awhile after their long trek. Later, she would dress suitably for dinner at Le Saint Benoit, one of Monte Carlo's top restaurants overlooking Grimaldi Rock. To follow up, they would pay a visit to the famous casino and try their hand at roulette. Herman, in a satisfied frame of mind, relaxed on deck with a lager and a Danish half-corona, observing the yachting activity out on the bay and mulling the idea of spending a million euros on a bronze sculpture. By his calculation, that was around $1,250,000, a tidy sum and more than he had ever spent on a single acquisition. It had better be worth the money, he considered.

To accompany his girlfriend this evening, he thought he would don his blue blazer, tailored slacks and country club tie. It was not often on this trip that they had been out on the town, preferring the more casual style of sidewalk cafes, Chinese take-aways and on-board grills. He would make the most of it, he decided, and introduce Nicola to the fine art of gambling, up to a limit of $2000. Who knew? She might even win.

CHAPTER 10

Olivier Breton woke early that day in his apartment at Pantin, the Paris suburb that was gradually gentrifying. He took a quick shower, dressed and prepared a leisurely breakfast of cereals followed by a Spanish omelet. He was in no particular hurry for a mid-morning meeting with Luc Picard. After relaxing over fresh coffee and yesterday's *Le Figaro* journal, he bestirred himself at nine o'clock, fed his parrot Asterix and strolled down the canal tow-path to the Metro. Alighting at Montmartre, noted for its sidewalk artists, he did some personal shopping before calling at Café Alfonse on Rue de l'Escargot. His contact was waiting for him, nursing an espresso with calvados while drawing on a Gauloise cigarette, whose pungent aroma pervaded the immediate vicinity. Breton sat down opposite him at the sidewalk table, ordering *café-au-lait*.

"*Ca va, Luc?*" he amicably enquired.

"*Ca va bien, Olivier, merci. Comment allez-vous?*"

"*Tres bien, aussi.*"

Pleasantries completed, they got down to serious business.

"According to your email, Luc, you have interesting news for me," Olivier Breton began.

"The bronze sculpture you asked me to keep an eye out for," the other replied, "has appeared on the market."

"In what manner?" the surprised agent asked.

"It is currently on display at Antichita di San Remo, with a price-tag of one million euros."

Olivier Breton returned a skeptical look.

"How could you know something like that," he asked, "when its whereabouts have so far been a complete mystery?"

Luc Picard gave an artful smile and took a long drag on his cigarette.

"The movements of a high-value object such as a Zodiac bronze cannot be kept hidden for long," he replied. "Practically the entire underworld is aware of it. It has been an open secret since the Irish mafia shipped it to Antwerp some days ago."

"The Irish mafia?" a curious Olivier Breton enquired. "Who exactly are they?"

"They style themselves the Erinesi. I have two names, Colm Byrne and Sean Scallan. They were tipped off about shipment of the sculpture from Glasgow to Cardiff by an employee of Siccurazione.sa, a freight insurer controlled by the Italian mafia."

"Who handled it from there?" the agent wanted to know.

"The Italians," Picard informed him. "Luigi Falconi, one of their art specialists, took charge of the transfer to the Riviera and then across the border into Italy. The rumor is that Falconi got it rather cheaply. The Irishmen had little sense of its true value."

Olivier Breton sat back in his chair and thoughtfully sipped his coffee. Eventually, he said:

"The business at San Remo, is that legitimate?"

"Antichita di San Remo is a firm of good repute. But you know as well as I do, Olivier, that art dealers, gallery owners and even museums do not always enquire too deeply into the provenance of the pieces they acquire. Prestige and profit often trump due diligence."

"That is true enough," the agent allowed.

"If you have a spare million," the other then said, "which I do not for one moment doubt, the bronze is yours for the asking."

Olivier Breton returned an enigmatic smile.

"The Directorate has its ways and means," he cryptically replied, passing a stuffed Manila envelope across the table.

Luc Picard opened it, quickly checked the contents and seemed satisfied.

"Always a pleasure to do business with you, *mon cher ami*," he said.

"Likewise," replied the agent, rising from his chair and bidding his contact adieu.

He then took the Metro to St. Germain-des-Pres, reaching the Directorate just as Louis Dutourd was about to leave for lunch. On spotting his agent, who seemed unusually up-beat, the director wanted to hear what he had to say. Lunch could wait.

"Take a seat," he said, inviting Breton into his office.

The agent sat facing his superior with a broad smile on his face.

"It is in the bag, Monsieur le Directeur," he announced.

"You mean to say that you have actually obtained the bronze?" an incredulous Louis Dutourd asked.

"As good as," came the reply. "One of my contacts in the underworld claims that it is now on sale at an antique dealership in San Remo."

"The Italian Riviera, indeed?"

"The price-tag is one million euros."

"Well done, Monsieur Breton!" the director said. "Now we can really steal a march on the Japanese, the Russians and anybody else who might have designs on it."

"It is a lot more straightforward than mounting a commando raid on a Russian freighter," Olivier Breton remarked.

Louis Dutourd gave a wistful sigh.

"Hardly as exciting," he said. "I discussed the possibility with the prime minister, who promised to give it some thought. I doubt, though, that in the end he would have approved the plan. There would have been an international outcry, had we been unmasked."

Reaching into his desk drawer, he took out a departmental book of checks, removed one, signed it and passed it to his agent.

"Fill in the appropriate amount on the spot," he advised, "in case you can bargain the price downwards. The dealer might be willing to go for a quick sale, to get it off his hands."

"I shall leave Paris tomorrow evening," Breton said, pocketing the blank check, "on the car-sleeper service to Nice. It will then be a comfortable drive down the coast to San Remo. "

On reaching his own office, he texted Yuki Kimura at Canary Wharf to tell her the good news.

*

Two days later, George Mason was down early for breakfast at Hotel Adler, in the old quarter of Zurich known as the Altstadt, with its narrow, cobbled streets and long flights of steps leading up to the Lindenhof. He joined the few early patrons for the warm buffet, pleased that he had opted to extend his stay in Switzerland. Since it was fine weather, he was contemplating a ferry cruise across the lake to Rapperswil, to follow up a funicular rail trip over the steep Brunig Pass the previous day. First, he had to call Bill Harrington, to bring the chief inspector fully up-to-date.

"Having a useful trip, Inspector?" Bill Harrington enquired.

"Not exactly what I expected," Mason replied. "But certainly quite useful."

"That lead Leutnant Kubler gave us was a bit vague, I agree. Didn't it work out as anticipated?"

"In fact, Chief Inspector, it led to a most remarkable discovery, but just not what we are looking for. Leutnant Kubler had me go down to Bellinzona to meet with a certain Professore Scarpa, who drove me to a villa north of the city. On entering the atrium, we were confronted by the bronze effigy of a snake in attack-mode. It looked so realistic in the half-light that I stopped dead in my tracks."

"You were scared!" Harrington said, with a loud guffaw.

"I was certainly taken aback," Mason admitted, "to say the least."

"Stone the crows, Inspector! Wait until I tell the superintendent about it. It will make his day."

"If you insist, Chief Inspector," the piqued detective replied.

"Was this snake you mention in any way related to the dog?" Harrington asked.

"It was indeed, Sir. Isidore Scarpa, an Orientalist at Academia del' Arte in Bellinzona, quickly determined that it was one of the missing Zodiac bronzes. The owner had grown chary about keeping it, in view of all the recent publicity in the media. He has decided of his own accord to return it to China."

"How does that concern us, Inspector?" his senior wanted to know.

"The owner is a Eurasian named Li Fournier," Mason explained. "He has asked us to contact the Chinese Embassy in London about it. I am hoping you can set that in motion, Chief Inspector, while I am taking two days of my accrued vacation time here. If we are instrumental in its return, it will put us in good stead with the Chinese authorities."

"Pigs' trotters, Inspector?"

"Why not, if the Scots can eat sheep's offal?"

"If pigs' trotter can help us out of our economic doldrums, well and good," Harrington said. "We might also promote the haggis to our Asian friends, now that you mention it. It would be a boon to our sheep farmers. I shall contact the Foreign Office right away. But you can forget about taking more of your vacation time."

"Why is that?" a concerned George Mason asked, sensing that his boat trip on Lake Zurich was now in jeopardy.

"Because there is a hot new lead from Europol," his senior said. "The Carabinieri have come across a bronze sculpture of a dog at San Remo. It looks like it could be the genuine article. They had their own expert, from the University of Genoa, validate it. You are to go there without delay and make contact with an Ispettore Gianni Baggio."

"You amaze me, Chief Inspector," Mason said. "Where exactly is the bronze located?"

"At an art dealer's named Antichita di San Remo, with a price-tag of one million euros. The Carabinieri will be awaiting your instructions, since it was illegally removed from Britain."

"I can leave almost at once," George Mason said, figuring that he could take the inter-city service from Zurich to Turin, with a direct connection to the Italian Riviera.

"Give it your best shot," his superior urged, ringing off.

*

Two days previously, Akira Issiguru received an unexpected telephone call at his rental apartment in Geneva, having quickly returned to Europe from Tokyo following his deportation from Britain.

"Good afternoon, Akira," came the friendly voice of Matsuo Yamoto.

"What a pleasant surprise," the special agent replied. "How are things with you?"

"Just fine, honorable friend. Listen closely. I have some interesting news for you."

"Good news, I trust?"

"Very good news, in fact. I confronted Yuki Kimura about a possible leak from this office. After pressuring her, she finally owned up to it. She could hardly do otherwise, since she was the only other person privy to my official telephone conversations. I trusted her implicitly."

"Rather lax of you, Matsuo, in the circumstances."

"It seems she has a contact in the French secret service."

"His name?"

"She would not divulge that, Akira. But in recompense for her disloyalty, she indicated that the French know the precise whereabouts of the Zodiac bronze."

"You cannot be serious, Matsuo!" Issiguru exclaimed.

"This is on the level, Akira. The bronze is on display at an art dealer's called Antichita di San Remo."

"You mean the Italian Riviera resort?"

"I know of no other."

"That is only a short flight from Geneva."

"Instead, Akira, you are to go to Monte Carlo as soon as possible. Our Noh theatre troupe is currently touring both the French and the Italian Rivieras. It will be good cover for you to join them as an extra. They are transferring to San Remo in two days' time."

"I can be there by tomorrow," the agent promised. "Have you dismissed Yuki?"

The director swallowed hard.

"I cannot bring myself to do that, Akira," he said. "She is of invaluable assistance to me on the Japanese language courses, and she has promised to break off all contact with the French agent."

"A weakness, Matsuo," the other cautioned. "But in view of the information you have just supplied, I shall choose to overlook it. I did not mention the likelihood of an internal leak at your cultural mission to my superiors at Tokyo, to spare you a degree of embarrassment."

"Very kind of you, esteemed colleague. I am deeply grateful."

"If her contact is the same person who confronted me at Criccieth, North Wales, he is one mean son-of-a-bitch."

"You may cross swords again, in Italy."

"An interesting scenario, Matsuo. Also, a very unpredictable one."

*

George Mason left Zurich shortly after his conversation with Bill Harrington and caught the mid-morning rail service to Turin. From there, he transferred to the Riviera Express, reaching the coastal city of San Remo by early evening. Police Headquarters were conveniently situated near the railway station. On entering, he was warmly greeted by Ispettore Gianni Baggio.

"Inspector George Mason, from Scotland Yard," the visitor said, introducing himself.

"We have been expecting you," the Italian officer replied, grasping his hand. "Let us go without delay to the dealer's showroom. His name is Vittorio Rossi."

"Has Rossi been notified of our interest in the bronze sculpture?" the detective asked, on their way out to the car.

"We thought it best to keep the matter low-key until you arrived, Inspector," came the reply. "Rossi has a good reputation in his field. He may not be aware that the sculpture was stolen."

"He may not have asked," Mason wryly commented.

"In our country," Baggio said, rather sardonically, "we are more used to art treasures leaving Italy than entering it. There is a big illicit trade in antiquities looted from archaeological sites, museums and even private villas. Not to mention paintings, rare books and manuscripts."

"I take your point, Inspector," Mason said. "You are sure the bronze is authentic?"

Gianni Baggio took a left turn into a narrow side-street, parked his car and said:

"No less a person than Dottore d'Adamo, of the University of Genoa, examined it and declared it genuine. He was amazed that such an item had turned up here on the Riviera."

"After a roundabout trip from Scotland?"

"Is that so, Inspector? That is truly amazing."

"It was originally brought to Europe by a colonel in a Scottish guards regiment, who took part in the Opium Wars."

"Quite a history, in that case, Inspector."

On entering Antichita di San Remo's premises, they were cordially greeted by the proprietor, Vittorio Rossi, who showed scant alarm at the appearance of a uniformed officer.

"What can I do for you gentlemen?" he asked.

"I am Ispettore Baggio, of the Carabinieri," the Italian officer announced. "And this is Inspector George Mason, of Scotland Yard Special Branch."

"Scotland Yard?" the astonished dealer repeated.

"We are here in connection with the bronze sculpture of a dog that Dottore d'Adamo examined at these premises the other day," Baggio said, glancing round the store. "But I do not see it."

"It has been sold," Rossi nonchalantly informed them, "to an American couple, less than one hour ago."

"Sold!" George Mason exclaimed.

"For a very good price," the well-satisfied dealer replied.

"Were you aware that it was stolen goods, Signore Rossi?" Ispettore Baggio asked.

The dealer returned an evasive look.

"It came from a reputable source," he said, shifting his stance uneasily.

"We shall look into that later," the Italian officer said. "Where is the bronze now?"

The dealer checked his records.

"It was shipped to the harbor, to a yacht called the *Teal*, owned by a gentleman named Herman Eades. Quite a legitimate transaction, I do assure you. Oddly enough, you are the second party to enquire about it since it left my showroom."

"The first being...?" an intensely curious George Mason prompted.

"He did not give his name, but I got the impression from his accent that he was from northern France, or possibly from Belgium."

George Mason's mind went back to an interesting encounter at Criccieth, North Wales, to the man who had identified a certain Japanese agent arrested for intruding on and harassing Vera Weeks. How curious that he should now re-enter the picture, he mused.

"We should go down to the harbor," Ispettore Baggio then said, "without delay. The yacht may be preparing to sail on the evening tide."

Leaving the store with a threat to the dealer of further enquiries, they sped down to the shore, parked on the quayside and quickly identified the *Teal* flying the Stars and Stripes. As they boarded the vessel, they were confronted by three individuals, two men and a younger woman. A large, slatted crate stood on the foredeck.

"What the hell is going on?" a bemused Herman Eades asked.

"Gianni Baggio, of the Carabinieri," the Italian officer said, introducing himself. "And this Inspector George Mason, of Scotland Yard."

The yachtsman and his partner returned incredulous glances, while the Frenchman gave a wry smile, on recognizing the English detective.

"We believe you just acquired one of the Zodiac bronzes," George Mason explained, indicating the wooden crate.

"I paid good money for it," the American replied. "And this French gentleman here has offered me half as much again."

"You should accept his offer, Herman," Nicola Montales urged.

"Unfortunately," Baggio said, "There can be no re-sale of this item. I am here to impound the sculpture, which was stolen from a British journalist about two weeks ago."

The yachting pair looked aghast.

"We paid a million euros for this piece of metal," Herman Eades remonstrated.

"Then I would advise you to negotiate with Vittorio Rossi about a re-fund," Baggio said. "The Carabinieri will back you up and help you obtain a court order, if necessary."

"What will happen to the bronze now?" a defeated-looking Olivier Breton asked. "Shall it be restored to the journalist?"

George Mason thought about that for a moment, recalling what Li Fournier had decided about the future destiny of the snake.

"I shall take advice on that issue from the Foreign Office," he informed him. "I am aware that the French would dearly wish to acquire it, so that they can eventually restore it to China, supplementing their gift of the rabbit and the rat earlier this year."

"You seem very well-informed, Inspector," an impressed Olivier Breton conceded, "about the activities of the French government. It is quite true that, as a gesture of goodwill, two of the Zodiac bronzes, acquired by a French businessman at auction, were returned to Beijing."

"But there seem to be other interested parties with their own objectives," the detective continued. "As I said, I shall take advice on the matter. Meanwhile, the Italian police will hold it in safe keeping."

"We have secure storage units for the purpose," Ispettore Baggio remarked, calling the police station by cellphone to make appropriate arrangements.

"What a fine kettle of fish this is," Herman Eades resignedly remarked.

"Herman was so looking forward to wowing the members of his country club," Nicola almost tearfully added.

"There will be other fish to fry, Nicola," her partner philosophically commented, extending his culinary metaphor. "Now, can I offer you folks a drink in this thirsty weather?"

"A great idea," George Mason said, "while we are awaiting removal of the bronze."

Nicola went below-deck to fetch beer or wine, as requested. Mason glanced towards the quayside, noting with interest the rather incongruous figure of an Asian wearing a floppy hat and an open-neck shirt standing a little distant from fellow anglers trying their luck on the incoming tide. To the detective's eye, he did not seem very adept, the awkward way he cast the line. At the same time, he seemed vaguely familiar. Turning to the Frenchman, he said:

"Have you noticed that curious individual fishing from the quay?"

Olivier Breton glanced briefly in that direction, just as Nicola re-appeared on deck. The drinks' tray immediately occupied their attention as, minutes later, a police van appeared on the scene. Four policemen alighted from it, receiving instructions from Ispettore Baggio to remove the crate and take it to a safe-storage unit. The remaining quartet sipped chilled lager or Valpolicella in the warm evening sunshine, not noticing the angler abandon his task, enter a Renault sedan parked nearby and head off in the same direction as the police van. Gianni Baggio gave his English visitor directions to the hotel he had pre-booked for the night, before the detective set off for a stroll round the harbor before dinner. The Italian officer then accompanied Herman Eades and Nicola Montales to Antichita di San Remo, to claim a refund.

*

Later that evening, Akira Issiguru entered the lobby of Hotel Camelia, where the Japanese theatre troupe was staying. He immediately placed a call to Matsuo Yamoto at his West London home.

"Good evening, honored friend," the mission director said. "What have you to report?"

"Yuki's information was correct," the agent eagerly replied. "The Zodiac bronze is right here in San Remo."

"Its precise location?" Yamoto enquired.

"I was able to observe its transfer aboard a yacht owned by an American couple. The Carabinieri are aware that it has been stolen and have removed it to a storage unit near the harbor."

"Very good work, Akira," the other said. "It will be a simple matter for someone with your professional training to effect entry to the unit and retrieve the sculpture. Take two of the strongest actors in the Noh troupe to assist you."

"How do we proceed after that?" Issiguru wanted to know.

"Disguise it as theatre equipment," came the reply. "Tomorrow, as you are aware, the troupe will move on to Ventimiglia, for their final engagement. When their tour is completed, a charter vessel, the *Roppongi*, will arrive in Ventimiglia to take on board all the crated theatre props. The Zodiac bronze will be indistinguishable from other items of equipment, safe from the prying eyes of the Italian authorities."

"An excellent plan, Matsuo," the agent commented. "But more than the Italian police are involved."

"What exactly do you mean by that, Akira?"

"The Frenchman Yuki tipped off about my mission in England is also here in San Remo. In addition, there is the British detective who had me arrested at Criccieth. He is staying at Hotel Mirafiori."

"If you make your move at night, esteemed colleague," Yamoto replied, "you need have no qualms about the French or the British. Our plan is watertight. Nobody would begin to suspect a classic theatre troupe. Once the bronze is aboard the charter vessel, we are home and dry."

"You have thought things through very thoroughly, Matsuo," the agent agreed. "It shall go as planned."

"We have Yuki to thank for this positive development," Yamoto said.

"She has redeemed herself, Matsuo, for the time being. In future, I would not keep her privy to your telephone conversations."

"She is well-aware that she is under a cloud," the other replied, "and will conduct herself accordingly. Enjoy your dinner."

"Veal cutlets with linguini and edamame is on the menu tonight at Hotel Camelia."

"I shall join you in spirit, my good friend," the other said.

CHAPTER 11

On rising the following morning, George Mason gazed out of the window of his hotel room, which overlooked San Remo bay, in time to watch the *Teal* maneuver from the quay and hoist sail as it veered towards the open sea. He felt some sympathy towards the American couple in their frustrated attempt to acquire a valuable piece of art and gave them a token wave, even though they would not be aware of the gesture. The previous evening, Herman Eades had mentioned that they were moving on to Madeira, to stock up on dessert wines. Too much sympathy for such wealthy persons – didn't Herman Eades say he was a potash billionaire? – seemed out of place, as he turned from the window, took a quick shower and went down to a breakfast of prosciutto and eggs Benedict. On eventually rising from the table, he placed a call to Bill Harrington.

"Enjoying the Riviera, Inspector?" came the ironic tones of the chief inspector.

"Weather is wonderful," Mason replied. "I am staying at a comfortable, modest hotel facing the sea."

"Lucky you, Inspector," the other returned. "It is pouring down here in London. How do you manage to land such attractive assignments?"

"Because you yourself requested it," Mason jocularly replied.

"From your up-beat tone of voice," his senior then said, "I gather that you are making progress in the case."

"It is all sewn up," Mason said. "The Zodiac bronze was retrieved last evening from a yacht skippered by a wealthy American named Herman Eades and secured in a police storage unit."

"Under guard, I trust?"

George Mason had wondered about that himself. Why hadn't Gianni Baggio specifically mentioned a police guard?

"The Carabinieri seemed to think it would be secure enough, Chief Inspector," Mason explained. "This city apparently has a low crime-rate."

"I shall take your word for that, Inspector," Bill Harrington replied, "even though Riviera resorts are certainly no strangers to thievery. "What are your plans now, might I ask, regarding the final destination of the bronze?"

"There are several interested parties," Mason replied. "The Russians, the French and the Japanese have all declared a strong interest in it."

"The Russians paid good money for it, Inspector, but there remains the question of an export license. Reliable sources at Whitehall tell me that the Home Secretary is unlikely to grant one in the immediate future."

"What about the funds they have disbursed?"

"Vera Weeks can reclaim her outlay from the insurance company," Harrington replied, "to avoid a diplomatic spat with Russia. I do not see how we can mediate the claims of three different parties. The Zodiac bronze must return to London, for the time being at least."

George Mason thought about that.

"I have a suggestion to make, Chief Inspector," he said, on sudden inspiration. "Why not refer the matter to UNESCO and let them make the decision. It will let Britain off a very tricky hook."

There was a pause at the end of the line, before the senior officer said:

"An interesting idea, certainly, Inspector. I shall start the process straight away. Shall I expect you back in London later today?"

"You are forgetting," Mason replied, "that I still have a couple of days' vacation left, having disrupted my visit to Switzerland."

"I expect you have earned it," Harrington generously allowed. "My sincere congratulations on your notable success!"

"Did you approach the Chinese regarding the snake?" Mason then asked him.

"The Foreign Office have been in touch with them. They are very pleased at the prospect of its return to China by Li Fournier. No mention has been made of the dog, so far. Enjoy the remainder of your stay, Inspector."

George Mason's euphoria, however, was short-lived. Relaxing in the hotel lounge after his breakfast, he was surprised to receive a visit from Ispettore Baggio. The Italian officer looked crestfallen.

"Our storage unit was broken into during the night," he gravely announced.

"The sculpture has disappeared?" the startled detective asked.

Baggio sank into an armchair and threw up his hands in despair.

"It is the last thing I anticipated," he said. "An expert job, too. What I do not understand is how the thieves could have known it was there."

George Mason rose from his chair and paced the room.

"Your officers," he said, "apart from the Eades themselves, were the only persons aware of the overnight arrangements for the piece. How reliable are they?"

The Italian officer returned a rather wounded look.

"I trust my junior officers implicitly," he said. "As for Herman Eades, who was very keen to own the sculpture, he obtained a full refund from Vittorio Rossi, in my presence."

"We must not overlook the Frenchman either," the detective interposed. "He had strong designs of his own."

"Olivier Breton returned to Paris on the overnight Riviera Express," Baggio said. "He informed me before he left that he had conferred with the Directorate in Paris. The French authorities will now confine their efforts to diplomatic channels."

George Mason sat down again and ordered fresh coffee, inviting his counterpart to join him.

"This is a real reversal, Inspector," he said. "I just rang my superior, Chief Inspector Harrington, to tell him that the case was sewn up."

"You have my sympathies, Inspector Mason," his Italian counterpart said. "We have recurring problems in Italy with stolen objets d'art, illegal excavations and outright forgeries."

The Englishman did the honors, pouring two cups of Java before settling back in his chair to collect his thoughts. After a while, he said:

"Have you noticed anything out of the ordinary here in San Remo, during the last few days?"

"The resort is full of tourists," came the reply, "so it is hard to pick out anything in particular, among all the new faces."

"You are sure that nothing comes to mind, Inspector?"

"Nothing out of the ordinary," came the reply, "except perhaps that a Noh theatre troupe recently arrived at Teatro di Liguria."

"Japanese theatre?" an immediately intrigued George Mason said. "Is there something extraordinary about that?"

"It is a first, in the history of San Remo, in so far as I am aware," Baggio replied. "My wife has always taken a strong interest in theatre. It was she who noted their arrival and mentioned it to me last evening over dinner."

A slow smile spread across his visitor's face, as he recalled the curious figure of an angler casting his line rather inexpertly from the quay, as he himself was aboard the *Teal*. A certain train of thought entered his mind.

"Come, Inspector," he said, draining his cup and rising to his feet. "Let us pay Teatro di Liguria a quick visit."

A perplexed Ispettore Baggio followed George Mason outside and drove him the short distance to the theatre. On entering, they noticed that the stills representing the Noh troupe were being removed from the foyer, to be replaced by stills illustrating an American troupe called Shakespeare Today. Gianni Baggio approached the person who seemed to be in charge.

"Has the Japanese troupe already moved on?" he enquired.

"Down the coast, to Ventimiglia," the official replied. "They open this evening at Teatro Contemporaneo, for two nights only, on the final leg of their European tour."

"Do you have any of the San Remo programs left?" George Mason asked.

The man nodded, stepped into the booking-office and returned with a small sheaf.

"Help yourself," he said.

"Just one copy will suffice," Mason said, immediately scanning the cast list, while vaguely recalling the name of a certain Japanese agent Olivier Breton had disclosed at Criccieth. None of the names on the list rang a bell, however. Turning to Gianni Baggio, he said:

"Have you ever watched a Noh play?"

"I do not believe I have," the Italian officer replied. "Not even on television."

"Now is your opportunity," his English counterpart said, with an artful smile.

"You mean, Inspector, that you want me to drive you down to Ventimiglia to watch Japanese theatre?" an intrigued Gianni Baggio asked.

"If it is not too far out of your way?"

"It is no great distance from here," the other replied. "About thirty minutes by car, depending on traffic. Since I am free this evening, after writing up my report on the recent theft, I shall be more than happy to accompany you to Ventimiglia. I could pick you up at your hotel at, say, five-thirty. There is a restaurant along the coast specializing in Tuscan dishes. We could have dinner there before the show."

"An excellent suggestion," the Englishman said, pocketing his Noh program. "I shall be waiting for you outside my hotel. Would your wife care to join us?"

"Silvia left first thing this morning to visit her sister at Stresa, on Lago di Maggiore. Otherwise, she would have jumped at the chance."

"You shall have to relay your impressions to her, in that case."

"She will be most interested," Baggio said, as he headed out towards his car. "*Arriverderci.*"

"*Arriverderci, Ispettore,*" Mason replied, in his best Italian.

Declining the offer of a lift, in favor of a little exercise, the detective strolled back down to the waterfront. Since no further progress in the case was possible for the time being, he opted to spend a relaxing afternoon at the beach, calling at the station kiosk on the way to buy a copy of *The Times.* It would be an opportunity to catch up on the news from England, including the latest cricket scores, and Stock Market trends for the portfolio of investments he had made towards his retirement. He eventually found a trattoria along the promenade, from where he placed a call to his wife Adele, to let her know everything was all right. He did not mention his new concerns.

At some point, he realized, he would also need to ring Bill Harrington, to apprise him of the setback in the case. The chief inspector was annoyed enough at the debacle on Elizabeth Dock, Cardiff. He would not be amused to learn that the sculpture had vanished yet again, this time from under the very noses of the Italian police. Mason was of no mind to call London today. Tomorrow, if his hunch about the Noh theatre troupe were to prove productive, would make much better sense.

Bang on time, Ispettore Gianni Baggio picked him up outside his hotel and drove several miles along the coast road before stopping at a family-owned restaurant in the picturesque village of San Giralomo. After a tasty meal of *pollo Toscana*, helped down with a shared bottle of Barolo, they arrived at Teatro Contemporaneo minutes before the performance was due to start. The auditorium was about half-full, with local people and tourists, as they entered to take their seats in the stalls. George Mason overheard English and American accents.

The official program gave an outline of the play in English as well as Italian, in an obvious nod to English-speaking tourists. It was sufficient for George Mason to vaguely follow the plot, centered on a celebrated swordsmith ordered to forge a new weapon for a nobleman. The audience seemed thoroughly to enjoy this novel and unfamiliar form of theatre, dating back hundreds of years. What mainly impressed the detective were the elaborate costumes, the chanting of the chorus and the vigorous action scenes. An enthralled Gianni Baggio leaned forward on the edge of his seat.

When the curtain went up for the final scene, staged outside a villa below Mount Inari, Mason could scarcely believe his eyes. As the mists cleared, a bronze effigy of a dog placed by the entrance to the villa slowly came into focus. He leaned forward and peered closely at it, across the short distance between the third row of the stalls and the stage, to ascertain if it resembled the piece he had seen on the deck of the *Teal*. Reasonably satisfied that it was the same piece, cunningly disguised as a theatre prop, he nudged his companion and pointed it out to him. Ispettore Baggio in turn gave the piece a long, hard look. His face lit up, as much in relief as in surprise, as he gasped aloud, causing people's heads to turn.

"You had an idea, Inspector, didn't you," he said in admiration, as they filed outside to regain the cool evening air, "that this is where we would find the bronze."

"A case of putting two and two together," a gratified George Mason replied. "When you mentioned Noh Theatre being in town, it set off a certain train of thought. The inept Asian angler standing on the quay not very far from the *Teal* was the key to it. He was well-placed to observe the activity aboard the yacht and the departure of the police van, which he immediately followed. The presence in town of a Japanese troupe struck me as possibly more than coincidence. I could not be certain, of course, which is why I asked you to accompany me to a performance."

"As shrewd a piece of detective work as ever I witnessed, Inspector," Gianni Baggio granted, "besides being a most entertaining evening."

"You enjoyed the play?"

"Very much so," the Italian replied. "I had my doubts at first, but I would not have missed it for anything. If they come this way again, I shall definitely bring Silvia along. She will be sorry to have missed the performance."

"What should our next step be," George Mason then asked, "according to your protocol?"

"I shall contact my colleagues here in Ventimiglia," Baggio informed him, "and have them place the sculpture in safe storage."

"Under close watch this time?" the detective prompted, with a touch of irony.

"That goes without saying, Inspector," Baggio assured him. "I shall have a twenty-four-hour guard detailed for the purpose."

His English counterpart gave a nod of approval, before adding:

"Have the local police vet thoroughly the members of the troupe, to identify an individual named Akira Issiguru. Examination of passports should do it. He will have a lot of explaining to do, I imagine, regarding forced entry into a police storage unit."

The young Italian officer returned a broad, knowing smile.

"You amaze me, Inspector Mason," he said. "No real need for you to tag along, unless you especially wish to do so."

"Why don't I sit right here," Mason said, indicating the trattoria next to the theatre, "and have a quiet drink, while you take care of the formalities?"

"An excellent idea, Inspector," the other agreed. "I shall call for you in about an hour. We can then make our way back to San Remo."

George Mason happily occupied a table outside the busy cafe, observing the activity in the immediate neighborhood, while sipping a chilled beer with a feeling of renewed vacation. It was a warm evening, with a cool breeze off the Mediterranean. As the restaurant was filling up after the theatre and cinema shows, the waiter asked him if he would mind sharing his table. Rather reluctantly, the detective agreed. An elderly man almost immediately occupied the seat facing him and ordered a half-bottle of wine.

"*Buona sera*," he said, in greeting.

"*Buona sera*," the detective replied, in his best Italian.

The man picked up his foreign accent at once.

"*Inglese*?" he asked.

George Mason nodded, sensing that he was about to be drawn into conversation, when he would have preferred the company of his own thoughts.

"You are visiting Ventimiglia?" the man asked, in a friendly tone of voice.

"Just for the evening. I came down from San Remo with someone who will join me in a short while."

If he hoped that remark would deter the man, he was mistaken.

"San Remo was once very popular with English authors," he said.

"Is that so?" George Mason enquired, his curiosity roused.

"Edward Lear, for example, the writer of nonsense verse, spent his last years there and is buried in one of the churchyards."

"How interesting," Mason said, warming to his table companion. "You seem well-versed in English literature."

"I taught the subject at the local high school for many years," the man replied, "before taking my retirement in 2010."

"Which explains your excellent command of the language."

The former teacher smiled at the compliment and contentedly sipped his wine for a few moments, quietly appraising his table companion.

"What other writers have connections with this area?" George Mason asked.

"Tobias Smollett," came the quick reply, "The Scottish poet and novelist."

"And the first person to advocate sea-bathing, I believe," the detective remarked.

"I was not aware of that. But if it is so, we owe him a debt of gratitude, considering how packed our beaches are today. Our major income comes from tourism. Tobias Smollett was one of our very first regular visitors, during the eighteenth century."

"He fell in love with the Riviera?"

"I think he did. He wrote that our women were more beautiful and more even-tempered than the women of Provence, just across the border."

George Mason smiled at that observation.

"I expect he had his reasons for saying so," he diplomatically replied.

Eventually, Gianni Baggio appeared on the scene, declining Mason's offer of a beer.

"Would you accompany me to the police station, Inspector?" he said, with a curt nod of greeting to the retired teacher.

"Would that be necessary?" the detective asked, loath to leave his engaging table companion.

"Akira Issiguru wishes to meet you," Baggio rather roguishly informed him.

George Mason rose from his chair and glanced in surprise at his Italian colleague.

"You have arrested him?" he asked, with a gleam in his eye.

"He was a member of the chorus for the Noh play!"

Saying that, he led Mason to his car and drove a short distance through the busy streets of Ventimiglia. On arrival at their destination, he ushered the detective into an interview room. The Japanese agent rose to meet him.

"Honorable sir," he said, with a short bow, "this is the second occasion we have crossed paths."

"The first time being at Criccieth, I believe," Mason matter-of-factly replied.

Issiguru nodded.

"I would like to present you with my compliments," he continued. "You have bested me on both occasions. I wish to acknowledge defeat in the spirit of good British sportsmanship, which I had occasion to observe during my years as a post-graduate student in London."

George Mason stared back at him for a few moments, in astonishment. Eventually, he said:

"Very civil of you, Mr. Issiguru. I appreciate it."

"I trust you enjoyed our national theatre," the other then said.

"Very much so, I assure you," came the reply.

Issiguru returned a half-smile and gave another short bow, before being led out to the cells. Mason, a wry look on his face, turned to Gianni Baggio.

"What was all that about, do you think?" he asked.

The Italian officer merely shrugged.

"He may be angling for lenient treatment," he said, "buttering you up like that."

"Or perhaps he imagines we are on the playing fields of Eton," Mason drily observed, "a school where values like good sportsmanship still prevail."

"A brilliant ruse, all the same," the Italian officer commented, "to use the bronze as a theatre prop. It fit the villa scene perfectly."

"They might easily have pulled it off, too," his companion said. "And that would have got me in very hot water. I shall buy you a stiff drink on the way back, Inspector, as a mark of gratitude."

As they turned towards the seafront to reach the coast road, they spotted a Japanese freighter, the *Roppongi*, approaching the quay.

"I would place a bet," George Mason said, "that Issiguru was intending to use that vessel to spirit away the bronze."

"You may well be right, Inspector," Gianni Baggio replied. "We rarely see freighters at Ventimiglia. The occasional cruise liner, maybe."

*

Two days later, George Mason took the Underground to Charing Cross and proceeded along the Strand towards Fleet Street. By prior arrangement, Vera Weeks and Irina Carmichael were waiting for him in the editorial offices of *The Sunday Post*.

"Glad you could make it, Inspector," Auberon Maclintock said, rising to greet him.

"I expect you have quite a story to tell," Irina said, very pleased to meet him again.

The detective occupied the chair offered him, glancing from one to the other gathered round the cluttered table, as fresh coffee was served. Formalities completed, he said:

"You have your scoop at last, Mr. Maclintock."

"And what a scoop it is," the editor replied. "It will boost our circulation no end."

"You are the only person fully *au fait* with this story, Inspector," Vera Weeks rather reluctantly observed. "Can you fill us in?"

Auberon Maclintock poised to take notes.

George Mason, quite enjoying his role, was in no hurry. He sipped the hot coffee, while declining the offer of biscuits.

"It all began, I believe," he said, "with the will of the descendant of an officer in a Scottish guards regiment."

"A colonel who took an active part in the Opium Wars," the editor added.

"And who looted a bronze sculpture from the Zodiac Fountain at the Imperial Summer Palace in Beijing," Irina Carmichael said.

"It was one of twelve pieces forming the Chinese Zodiac," her sister added, "which I purchased at Arklet Studio, Inversnaid, on behalf of the Russian consulate."

"You reclaimed the money from Siccurazione.sa, Vera?" Mason asked.

"The claim is pending," came the terse reply.

"You then shipped the bronze to Cardiff with a freight service operating out of Glasgow," George Mason then said. "But it was intercepted en route by the Irish mafia."

"How could you know something like that, Inspector?" Vera Weeks challenged.

"They were in league with the Italian mafia," the detective replied. "The sculpture eventually reached San Remo, on the Italian Riviera. A dealer there, named Vittorio Rossi, was charged with receiving stolen goods. He, in turn, named his underworld contact, an individual named Luigi Falconi. The latter, hoping for more lenient treatment, showed little hesitation in naming his Irish contacts, a certain Colm Byrne and an associate whose name eludes me for the moment. The Garda are looking into the matter."

"You traced the sculpture to Italy?" an impressed Auberon Maclintock asked.

"With the assistance of the Carabinieri," Mason replied. "It was bought by a potash billionaire from Arizona, who was intent on expanding his private collection to include Oriental art. The first time I set eyes on the piece was aboard his yacht, the *Teal*, in San Remo harbor."

"You have had quite an adventure," Irina admiringly remarked.

"You can say that again!" the detective replied.

"So it was successfully recovered from the yacht?" the editor asked.

"The Italian police placed it in overnight storage," George Mason said. "However, the storage unit was broken into during the same night."

"You discovered the culprits?"

George Mason glanced at the investigative journalist.

"My biggest surprise in all this was to meet again with our Japanese acquaintance from Briar Cottage, Criccieth."

"You don't say so, Inspector!" an astonished Vera Weeks exclaimed.

"Akira Issiguru was – can you imagine? - disguised as a member of the chorus for a Noh troupe touring the Riviera. The Zodiac bronze was very realistically used as a theatre prop, but the agent had evidently not counted on Gianni Baggio and me attending a performance."

"What prompted you to attend the play?" Irina Carmichael asked.

"While aboard the *Teal*," The detective replied, "I spotted an Asian gentleman fishing very inexpertly from the quay. He looked vaguely familiar, but it is often difficult to tell one Asian from another. It was only when Ispettore Baggio mentioned a touring Japanese theatre company passing through the Riviera, that it suddenly struck me who the clumsy angler was."

"A remarkable story, Inspector Mason," Auberon Maclintock enthusiastically observed. "It will make great copy for next Sunday's edition."

"Where is the bronze now?" Vera Weeks wanted to know.

"And what is to become of it now?" her sister echoed.

George Mason drained his coffee, cleared his throat and said:

"It is now in safe storage at Ventimiglia. This time under close guard. I discussed the matter with Chief Inspector Bill Harrington at Scotland Yard this morning. Since there are several different countries seeking to own the piece, each with for its own purposes..."

"What purposes were those?" the editor brusquely interrupted.

"That is something I can only surmise," Mason continued, "and it is not my remit to do so, except to say that several countries wish to acquire it in order, I believe, to enhance their standing with China. In these rather complex circumstances, the Foreign Office decided to refer the decision regarding the final home of the Zodiac bronze to UNESCO."

"With what result?" Vera Weeks petulantly asked.

"In Geneva, they decided to return the sculpture to China, as the legitimate owners. A Royal Navy frigate, currently on exercises in the Mediterranean, will load it on board at Ventimiglia within the next few days."

Auberon Maclintock judiciously nodded, indicating his full agreement.

"The Chinese, at least, will be very gratified," Vera Weeks remarked.

"Not only on account of a bronze effigy of a dog," George Mason remarked.

All eyes turned expectantly towards the Scotland Yard visitor.

"In the course of my enquiries," he told them, "I came across a second Zodiac bronze."

"Which was?" they all asked in chorus.

"The snake!" Mason triumphantly announced.

A gasp went round the small assembly, as they glanced from one to the other in sheer amazement.

"How on earth did you accomplish that, Inspector?" the editor asked.

"It is a long story," the detective replied, not wishing to dwell on a rather unnerving experience at Villa Serena near Bellinzona. "Suffice it to say, for the moment, that it too will be returned to its rightful owners by a civic-minded individual living in Ticino."

"Truly remarkable, Inspector," Irina Carmichael said, with a look of unveiled admiration.

"It would make an excellent follow-up story for our newspaper," Maclintock eagerly prompted, "if you should at some future date feel inclined to relate it."

George Mason rose to take his leave.

"I shall give it careful consideration," he replied, on reaching the office door.

*

On arrival back at police headquarters, George Mason was warmly greeted by Chief Inspector Harrington.

"My congratulations, Inspector," the senior man said, "on your successful conclusion of the case. Andrew Forshaw just rang through from the Foreign Office to say that Sir David Finch is very pleased with the outcome and commends you for it."

"In that it will help promote British exports?" Mason promptly asked.

"Among other considerations, Inspector. But let us not be too mercenary. We shall be restoring to the Chinese a significant part of their cultural patrimony, removed by European troops over a hundred years ago. It may also help stimulate Chinese investment in some of our major infrastructure projects."

"I am very pleased to have contributed, in my small way, to such a satisfactory outcome," George Mason said.

"Do not underestimate yourself, Inspector," Bill Harrington protested. "You played a very significant role in the recovery of the bronze."

Mason was pleased to bathe for the moment in the high regard of his superior. The chief inspector had never been over-generous with his compliments.

"There is a new angle to this matter I want you to look into," Harrington then said.

"What would that be, Chef Inspector?" George Mason guardedly asked.

"I want you to direct your attention from effigies of living creatures to the real thing. The Irish police have arrested Colm Byrne and Seamus Scallan for their part in the theft. They suspect that the Erinesi are heavily involved in the illegal trade in animal parts."

"I was aware that the pair had stolen rhinoceros horns from museums," his colleague said.

"The Garda seem to think their activities may extend well beyond that. Much of the illicit trade in animal parts goes through North America, and on from there to destinations in the Far East. A portion of it will inevitably go through British ports, Inspector, and I want you to be our point man with the Irish authorities."

George Mason sat back in his chair and pondered his senior's remarks.

"I really know very little about wildlife, Chief Inspector," he confessed.

Bill Harrington returned an indulgent smile, saying:

"Make it your business to find out, Inspector. As a matter of fact, I have taken the first step for you. I made an appointment for you at ten o'clock tomorrow morning at the premises of Wildlife Concern, Shoreditch. The director, appropriately named Arthur Wildgoose, will give you a brief overview of the situation before he leaves for a conference at Geneva."

"I shall report to Shoreditch first thing tomorrow morning," Mason assured him, as he rose to leave.

He was scheduled to pick up Adele after her shopping trip to the West End. As a regular donor to the Humane Society, she was gratified to learn of this new development

The following morning, he duly presented himself at the address Bill Harrington had given him. Arthur Wildgoose received him cordially in his private office. While the wildlife expert briefly dealt with a telephone enquiry, the detective glanced round the room. It was very spare, with a filing cabinet, a bookcase and a mineral water dispenser. Posters of some of the world's most endangered animals hung on the far wall.

Having concluded his telephone business, Arthur Wildgoose sat back in his swivel-chair and quickly appraised his visitor.

"I understand from Chief Inspector Harrington," he began, "that you would like some background on the sort of work we do here."

"A brief overview of the matter," his visitor prompted, "so as not to take up too much of your time."

Arthur Wildgoose emitted a deep sigh and leaned forward in his chair, hands clasped.

"The problem, I regret to say, has many aspects, Inspector," he said. "A major one is bush meat. Elands and similar antelopes, along with smaller mammals, are a key source of food in sub-Saharan Africa."

"Not much has changed then," George Mason remarked, "since the days of the hunter-gatherers. If the practice has been going on for thousands of years, is it likely to stop any time soon?"

The director raised his eyebrows at that perceptive comment.

"It will indeed, as you suggest," he replied, "be very difficult to alter long-established ways of life. Great strides, however, are being made in various regions of the continent to improve agriculture, by introducing more modern methods. We can only hope such positive developments will decrease dependency on bush meat as a significant dietary source."

"What about the larger species we often hear about, as being in danger of extinction?" the detective then asked.

"The rhinoceros is a major concern, Inspector. During the last century there were tens of thousands of both black and white rhinos. At the present time, there are estimated to be fewer than five thousand left."

"What accounts for such a drastic decline, Mr. Wildgoose?" his concerned visitor asked.

"Rhinoceros horn," came the reply, "is considered by some peoples in the Far East to be a cure for cancer. Crushed rhino horn – you may find this hard to believe - is worth more than its weight in gold."

A light went on in Mason's brain at that remark. It fully explained why Colm Byrne and his associate Seamus Scallan found it worth their while to steal body parts from museums, an enterprise that had previously struck him as bordering on the farcical.

"Is there any scientific basis for such medicinal benefits, Director?" he asked

"None whatsoever," Wildgoose ruefully replied. "But it is extremely difficult to debunk established myths. Similar misconceptions apply to tiger parts."

"Another threatened species, I believe?" Mason said.

"Quite so, Inspector. Tiger testicles are claimed in traditional Oriental medicine to increase virility. Again, there is no scientific evidence whatsoever to support this belief."

"So wild animals are being killed for one supposedly vital part," his visitor remarked, "much as the shark has been hunted simply for its fins?"

"At least the authorities have been able to clamp down to some extent on that practice," the director said. "Even the Chinese seem to be getting on board. But the list goes on, Inspector. The steady increase in the price of ivory provides a powerful incentive to poachers. Elephant populations have decreased by around fifty per cent since the start of this century."

"This is an appalling situation, Mr. Wildgoose."

"You can say that again, Inspector. And you can appreciate that we have our work cut out here at Wildlife Concern, campaigning on behalf of threatened species, educating the public, pressuring politicians and making representations to governmental bodies. Now, if you will excuse me, Inspector Mason, I have a plane to catch. "

"Glad you could fit me in at such short notice," Mason said, rising to his feet.

"Do not mention it, Inspector Mason," Arthur Wildgoose said. "I am only too pleased that the Metropolitan Police are renewing their interest in the problem."

"We shall hopefully be able to play some small part in the conservation of wildlife, as the opportunity arises," the detective assured him.

"Meanwhile, Inspector," the director said, "since I am unable to remain with you longer, my assistant, Judith

Chalmers will introduce you to some of the key aspects of our work, including some of our more notable successes."

Saying that, he pressed a button on his desk, summoning an attractive young woman with shoulder-length auburn hair to his office. Introductions were made before Arthur Wildgoose quickly exited, leaving his visitor in the capable hands of the assistant.

"I should like to know," George Mason asked, intent on showing an intelligent interest in the subject, "what the qualifications are for conservation work."

"Usually a degree in biology or zoology," Judith Chalmers replied, "especially if it includes field work."

"You mean trips to the Galapagos Islands and suchlike?"

The young woman returned an indulgent smile.

"Nothing so exotic as that," she replied. "I obtained my degree at University College, here in London. It was a four-year course, with two semesters spent in California researching the San Joaquin kit fox."

"A threatened species?" the visitor asked.

Judith nodded.

"Its numbers are down over fifty percent," she informed him, "owing to loss of grassland in the Central Valley, its main habitat."

"What accounts for that, Judith?" he asked.

"The expansion of farming, as well as increased industrial and residential development."

"Fascinating," the detective said. "So what are you working on currently?"

"British butterflies," she promptly replied. "Their numbers are declining for a variety of reasons. I am particularly interested in the effects of climate change."

Saying that, she led him to a large workroom resembling a laboratory, at the rear of the premises, where he spent an interesting hour learning various aspects of conservation work. On arrival back at Scotland Yard shortly after midday, he reported to Bill Harrington, after exchanging a few words with Detective Sergeant Aubrey in the general office.

"A useful morning, Inspector?" the senior officer asked.

"Very useful, Chief Inspector," his colleague replied. "It was an eye-opener, in fact. Poaching of wildlife, whether for financial gain or for supposed medical benefits, is far more widespread than I had ever imagined."

"You may be able to put your evident concern to some good practical use, Inspector," Bill Harrington then said.

George Mason reacted in some surprise.

"In what way, Chief Inspector?" he tentatively enquired.

"While you were over in Shoreditch, I received a call from the Garda. Colm Byrne is turning state's evidence in the Dublin High Court, in the hope of receiving a more lenient sentence."

"Quite a break-through," Mason observed. "Has he already spilled the beans?"

"He has already said that a shipment of body parts is on the way from a West African port to Cork, in the Irish Republic," his senior informed him. "The Erinesi apparently have a storage depot at Cork Harbor, from where they make periodic shipments to the Azores by fishing vessel. Their associates in Boston take over from there, unloading the cargo on the U.S. eastern seaboard.

They then arrange its transfer to the West Coast, and on from there across the Pacific to markets in the Far East."

"Most interesting," Mason remarked. "But where exactly do I fit into all this?"

"The Irish police have invited you over to Cork to observe their procedures," Harrington explained. "The reason they gave was that the Erinesi may from time to time vary their choice of European port to avoid detection. They will likely use minor British ports on the Irish Sea, such as Fleetwood or Heysham. This is a trade with many ramifications, Inspector, on a world-wide scale. We may be able to tackle only a small fraction of it."

"If we can make any dent in it all, it will be worthwhile," Mason opined.

"I am glad you see it that way, Inspector. Why not take your wife with you and spend a few days in the area? It will help make up for the vacation time you forfeited in Switzerland."

"You bet, Chief Inspector!" a gratified George Mason exclaimed, thinking how Adele would just love to accompany him for once on one of his foreign assignments.

Made in the USA
Columbia, SC
24 March 2018